Buttons and Bones

Monica Ferris

BERKLEY PRIME CRIME, NEW YORK

THE BERKLEY PUBLISHING GROUP
Published by the Penguin Group
Penguin Group (USA) Inc.
375 Hudson Street, New York, New York 10014, USA
Penguin Group (Canada), 90 Eglinton Avenue East, Suite 700, Toronto, Ontario M4P 2Y3, Canada
(a division of Pearson Penguin Canada Inc.)
Penguin Books Ltd., 80 Strand, London WC2R 0RL, England
Penguin Group Ireland, 25 St. Stephen's Green, Dublin 2, Ireland (a division of Penguin Books Ltd.)
Penguin Group (Australia), 250 Camberwell Road, Camberwell, Victoria 3124, Australia
(a division of Pearson Australia Group Pty. Ltd.)
Penguin Books India Pvt. Ltd., 11 Community Centre, Panchsheel Park, New Delhi—110 017, India
Penguin Group (NZ), 67 Apollo Drive, Rosedale, North Shore 0632, New Zealand
(a division of Pearson New Zealand Ltd.)
Penguin Books (South Africa) (Pty.) Ltd., 24 Sturdee Avenue, Rosebank, Johannesburg 2196,
South Africa

Penguin Books Ltd., Registered Offices: 80 Strand, London WC2R 0RL, England

This book is an original publication of The Berkley Publishing Group.

This is a work of fiction. Names, characters, places, and incidents either are the product of the author's imagination or are used fictitiously, and any resemblance to actual persons, living or dead, business establishments, events, or locales is entirely coincidental. The publisher does not have any control over and does not assume any responsibility for author or third-party websites or their content.

FIRST EDITION: DECEMBER 2010

Library of Congress Cataloging-in-Publication Data

Ferris, Monica.
    Buttons and bones / Monica Ferris.—1st ed.
        p.   cm.
    ISBN 978-0-425-23704-5 (hardcover)
    1. Devonshire, Betsy (Fictitious character)—Fiction.   2. Needleworkers—Fiction.   3. Women
detectives—Minnesota—Fiction.   4. Dwellings—Remodeling—Fiction.   5. World War,
1939–1945—Prisoners and prisons, American—Fiction.   6. Germans—Minnesota—Fiction.
7. Prisoners of war—Fiction.   8. Minnesota—Fiction.   I. Title
    PS3566.U47B88   2010
    813'.54—dc22   2010029310

PRINTED IN THE UNITED STATES OF AMERICA

10   9   8   7   6   5   4   3   2   1

Acknowledgments

I want to thank Rita Mays for allowing me to use her wonderful log cabin as the model for the one purchased by Jill and Lars Larson in this book. There really is a Thunder Lake shaped like a duckling up in Cass County, Minnesota. My writers group, Crème de la Crime, again proved invaluable in their critiques of this manuscript as it was being written. The Longville and Ridgedale Public Libraries were helpful and valuable sources of information on the German POWs in the upper Midwest, as were Lucille Anderson and Helen Slagle. I want to thank Kevin Tschida, Donny "Swede" Hendrickson, and Rungwell Johanssen, coffee drinkers, for inspiring the set of characters at The Lone Wolf. Investigator Robert Stein of the Cass County Sheriff's Department answered lots of questions. My own dentist, Dr. Wallace Lunden, told me the difference between maxillary and mandibular molars. Tom Goodpaster of Blue Heron Investigations told me how he'd go about finding a missing person. Violet Putnam McDonald and Wilma Griffin are real people, but Betsy's conversations with them are fiction.

Buttons and Bones

One

MINNESOTANS refer to any lake in the state as *the* lake. Since there are actually more than the advertised ten thousand, this can be confusing.

"Say, I heard the Larsons went and bought that cabin up on the lake they were looking at," Phil said during the crochet class at Crewel World. He was referring to a cabin on Thunder Lake in Cass County.

Claudia's mother said, "Yes, they did. They're going to love it. A cabin up at the lake is the greatest place on earth to take kids during the summer." She was thinking of her own happy childhood at her parents' cabin on Long Lake near Litchfield.

Meryl's mother said, "We're going up to the lake this weekend," meaning Lake Hubert up near Brainerd.

Betsy, owner of the shop, said nothing, although Jill had kept her abreast of the purchase, as well as the first couple of visits to the cabin.

Betsy was co-presiding over a Saturday morning class called Crochet for Kids. Five mothers were present with six children—Claudia, nine, was there with her seven-year-old brother, Andrew.

The children were going to make "cup covers," double crochet roundels with lacy edges weighted with beads. They were meant to sit on top of opened cans of soft drinks or glasses of lemonade at outdoor picnics to keep the yellow jackets out of them.

The students had begun by making a chain. Lottie was the best at that—her chain grew over a yard long and gained speed with every stitch during that part of the lesson. Andrew was close behind, but poor Chloe couldn't even master How to Hold the Hook. Of course, she was only three and really wouldn't have been accepted in the class at all if her mother hadn't been a good customer and very insistent.

Now they were learning to make a round shape in single crochet. Little fingers thrust the size G hook through loops of worsted yarn, to drape the yarn over it, snag it, and draw it through. Little tongues appeared in the corners of small mouths, and the occasional high-pitched sigh or groan or giggle was heard.

And over the children's heads, the adults gossiped.

"Someone told me it's a real log cabin, a hundred years old," said Lottie's mother.

"Then they had better brace the walls," said Chloe's mother. "A hundred years of wood borers can turn logs into paper lace."

"I heard it doesn't even have indoor plumbing," offered Violet's mother. "Violet, darling, try using your left finger, instead of your thumb. That's right." She gave the teacher a look of rebuke for making her correct Violet herself.

Teacher Godwin, who was also the store manager, turned the look aside with a sweet smile. His method of teaching was to tell once, show once, and then wait for the pupil to ask for assistance. Violet had been managing quite well using her thumb.

"It has indoor plumbing," said Lottie's mother. "Jill told me that herself just last week, although they haven't got the water pump up and running yet."

"I hear the place is a wreck, that it stood empty for a lot of years," said Phil. An older man, without a child or grandchild accompanying him, Phil was himself a student. A knitter and needlepointer, he was seeking to add crochet to his needle working skills, and too impatient to wait for an adult class. He was using a heavy yarn and a big hook, suitable for his thick fingers and antique vision. He annoyed Betsy by adding, "Right, Betsy?"

She said, "I've heard something like that," and gave Phil a shushing grimace.

Betsy did not wish to be drawn into the discussion because she'd done something against one of her own rules, and helped Jill and Lars acquire the property.

Some years back, along with the shop, she had inherited a small company called New York Motto. The company, established in Wisconsin and run by a partner, searched out and bought houses and small businesses whose owners had gone bankrupt. It could be seen as a sad thing, battening on to other peoples' misfortune, and Betsy didn't care to get into a discussion of it.

It wasn't a difficult business to run, though it took some judgment to decide what properties to buy. The trick was finding them. Not many people knew where to look for these court-ordered bankruptcy sales, as they were usually advertised in obscure legal newspapers. Betsy's partner in New York Motto was a former paralegal who had worked for a firm specializing in monetary matters. After years of experience, her judgment was honed to a fine edge. All she needed was the capital, which Betsy's sister—and now Betsy—supplied. Once purchased, sometimes for pennies on the dollar, New York Motto would inspect the properties, sometimes do minor repairs, then use the Internet and ordinary newspapers to advertise and sell them at a profit.

In good times and bad, New York Motto was one of Betsy's more reliable sources of income; it was the reason she did not have to draw a salary on the profits from her needlework shop. Hardly any of Betsy's friends or acquaintances knew about the company, and Betsy was reluctant to share for several reasons, one being that some might want Betsy to give them a special deal.

Jill Cross Larson was an exception, though—and while she hadn't asked Betsy outright to help find her and Lars a bargain in lakefront property, they'd talked about the search she and Lars were conducting in language Betsy took as a hint.

So Betsy had started paying attention to buys the company was making on lakefront property well outside the Twin Cities, and when she found a couple of prospects, she let Jill know about them.

One, six acres with an old log cabin on it, was the more distant, three hours from Excelsior, only two from far-north Lake Itasca, source of the Mississippi River. The property came into bankruptcy court when the last legal owner fell into a terminal illness and mortgaged the place—long unused—to pay for medical expenses. He was, of course, unable to make payments.

The property was in a State Forest and on the shore of long, narrow Thunder Lake. Lars, experienced in buying and restoring property, drove up with Jill for a look and declared it a perfect location and the cabin suitable for restoration. Betsy took Lars's word for it and directed her partner to sell it to the Larsons with the caveat "as is."

On the other hand, since Jill was Betsy's best friend, Betsy sold it to them for what the company had paid for it.

But now, because she was not anxious to start a stampede of requests or rebukes, she allowed the gossip and speculation at the crochet class to wash over her without comment.

Betsy was attending the class because she, too, wanted to expand into crochet. She'd bought a couple of books on how to do it but, as usual, found she needed to actually sit in the presence of people who already knew how and watch how their fingers moved.

She could make a chain, slip stitch, and single and double crochet, after a fashion; that is, slowly and painfully, and with the instruction book propped up in her line of sight. What she couldn't do was crochet in a circle. It was like back when she could knit but not purl. Reading the instructions didn't help, even when they were accompanied by illustrations. Nor could she hold the yarn properly in her left hand. She'd wrap it around her little finger, bring it up and over her index finger, and set off, and within four or five stitches the yarn would have slipped off her fingers. Though it was currently easier to crochet this way, she knew that if she was to advance in the craft, she had to learn to do it properly.

Despite his lackadaisical attitude toward beginners, instructor Godwin agreed that Betsy needed to do it right. Talking to her earlier in the week, he had compared it to his golf game: At first he swung at the ball any old way and was happy to reach the green in six to nine strokes. And that was fine—at first. But to get into really playing, lowering his score, and breaking a hundred, he had to learn the odd stances and peculiar movements of the game, practicing them until they became natural.

So Betsy watched Godwin's hook flashing at top speed as it pulled yarn through the fingers of his left hand for a few moments. Then she gamely rewrapped the yarn through her own fingers and continued circling around her cup topper in single crochet—it had turned out that joining two ends and continuing to circle was far easier than holding the yarn properly.

"I heard they're going to tear down the log cabin and build a year-round residence—and then move up there permanently." This tidbit was offered by Meryl's mother.

Since Lars was a sergeant on Excelsior's little police department, a job he loved, Betsy doubted that very much. But she bit her tongue, thrust the crochet hook through a stitch, and reached for the yarn with her hook. She pulled it through so there were two loops on her hook, reached for the yarn again, and pulled it through both loops.

All those loops and it was called single crochet!

Of course it was a very solid, attractive stitch. Betsy looked at it admiringly. Just a few hundred more and she'd have a cup topper of her very own.

Two

Betsy was humming to herself as she closed up the shop. Connor was taking her out to dinner at a nice restaurant in Wayzata. She was pleasantly aware that things between the two of them were moving nicely; tonight he was going to bring his adult daughter Peg along to meet her.

Her smile grew complacent as she thought about Connor. He was very much her type: tall without being towering, strong without being muscle-bound, good-looking without being a true hunk. He had a keen mind, a sweet smile, and a wicked twinkle in his eyes. A retired Merchant Marine captain, he had a store of tales of life at sea that she found, in turn, moving or hilarious or exciting. Betsy, a former Navy WAVE, had always been attracted to things nautical.

Even better, Connor seemed to find a divorcee who was not tall or gorgeous or brilliant just his type. Maybe it was because his first wife had been all of those things, and it had not been a happy marriage. Betsy had been startled when he showed her a photograph of the first Mrs. Sullivan, who was a real beauty.

So maybe he was only pretending to court Betsy because she was his landlady and he was going to try for a reduction in his rent—she chuckled at the idea; he seemed to have all the money he needed to live comfortably, if not expansively. He had taken the smaller of the two rental units in her building last year, not because that was all he could afford but because that was all he needed. He had been born in Ireland, though his accent was, if anything, vaguely British at times.

A naturalized citizen of the United States, he had moved from Boston to Excelsior because his only daughter was in a graduate program at the University of Minnesota, and he wanted to be near her. She had been drawn to the university by a famous forensic anthropologist—her field of graduate study was biological anthropology.

And that gave rise to her sole worry about him. It appeared Peg was the only member of his immediate family still on friendly terms with him. His two sons had sided with their mother when the divorce finally happened, and though it had gone through five years ago, there were still hard feelings.

Betsy claimed she understood the family divided against itself, and she did, though not completely. She had no children from her two marriages, but while she might have no residual ill feelings about her first brief marriage, after all these years she still thought of her second husband as Hal the Pig.

She hoped the daughter was pleasant to know. The fact

that Connor was ready to introduce the two of them was an excellent sign.

She had just finished running the credit card machine when the door sounded its two-note warning that someone was coming in. She looked around, prepared to greet Connor, and saw instead an ethereally beautiful young woman with alabaster skin and smoky black wavy hair. She was very slim, with long legs encased in denim. She wore low-heeled sandals and a sleeveless silk blouse in a shade of green that exactly matched her eyes. But her full mouth turned down at the corners, and a frown made a tiny crease between her flawless brows. She looked to be in her early twenties.

Betsy was so taken aback by her that she didn't notice at once that Connor had come in on her heels. He spoke first. "Betsy, I want you to meet my daughter, Margaret Rose Sullivan. Peg, this is my very dear friend, Betsy Devonshire."

Wow, thought Betsy. She extended her hand. "How do you do?"

"How do you do?" replied the young woman, not taking the hand. She turned to her father. "Well, Da, she's just as you described her." She had a lovely, lilting Irish accent.

"Are you about done here?" Connor asked Betsy.

"Just a few more minutes," promised Betsy.

"I hope so. I skipped lunch and I'm really starving," said Peg.

Betsy kept her promise, and in five minutes they were in Connor's car, heading up Highway 15 toward Orono. It skirted big Lake Minnetonka with its many bays and small towns along the way.

"The lake is beautiful," said Peg. "How big is it?"

"There are a hundred miles of lakeshore," said Betsy.

"Oh, it's even bigger than I thought."

"Yes, it's so convoluted that it's hard to take the whole thing in, except from the air."

Peg went on, in a tone that hinted of amused condescension. "Everything around here is named with the syllable *Mini*, as if it's small, even things like this grand, huge lake."

"*Minne* is an Indian word for 'water,'" said Betsy. "Minnetonka, Minnewashta, Minneapolis, even Minnesota, which means 'many waters.' There are a *lot* of lakes in the state."

"I see. Da, do you like living here? I mean, this is kind of a backwater place . . ." She laughed. "I mean, it's hardly New York or Los Angeles. I came here because of Professor Henry Lamb at the university, and I'll be gone in two years. Will you be glad to leave, too?"

Backwater? Humph! But Betsy found herself holding her breath while waiting for his reply.

"You know the reason I came here was to live near you. But I'm finding another reason, and she's not leaving in two years." Connor's baritone was as warm as it was certain, and Betsy, sitting in the backseat, felt a thrill at this near declaration of intent.

"I see," said Peg thoughtfully, and she gave a swift, not altogether friendly glance into the backseat.

THE restaurant in Wayzata was very nice.

"Is that how you say it, Why-ZET-ta?" asked Peg, while they waited to be seated. "Another Indian name, I suppose, written down by semiliterate settlers."

Betsy said, "It is Indian. *Waziya* is the name of the Sioux god of the north, he who blows the cold north wind from his mouth. The suffix *ta* means 'shore,' and the whole just means 'North Shore.' Lake Minnetonka was very sacred ground to this Mdewakanton branch of the Dakota or Sioux. I don't think the spelling is illiterate, I think the difference between the spelling and pronunciation is a product of scholars, the same sort who keep changing the spelling and pronunciation of Chinese place names."

Peg laughed. "*Touché*," she said.

Betsy said, "I hope you are getting all you want from your studies at our university."

"Oh, yes—well, at least as much as I expected from a redbrick college."

Betsy took a breath to reply, then bit her tongue. Connor's ears were turning red, his sign of annoyance. No need to aggravate him further. But she wondered what had Peg's undies all in a twist.

"Now, Peg," said Connor, "many of these 'redbrick' universities are doing extremely good work. You came here yourself specifically to work with Dr. Lamb, who obviously is himself satisfied with the University of Minnesota."

"Yes, of course you're right, Da," said Peg meekly.

Betsy had never heard a parent called "Da" except in British movies, but thereby knew it was a common Irish term of endearment for a father. She was touched by this evidence of a close tie of affection and respect between Connor and Peg. Betsy hoped Peg didn't see her as a threat to the tie between the two of them. She would have to step very carefully.

Connor said to Betsy, "Has Jill Larson asked you up to their cabin yet?"

"Yes, but I can't get away right now. Besides, I think they were just being polite. They've got a lot of work to do before it's presentable for company."

"Maybe they're hoping to organize a working party."

Betsy laughed. "That could be."

"Who's Jill Larson?" asked Peg. "And why do you use a plural noun when speaking of her?"

Connor said, "She's married to Lars Larson . . ." Peg snorted. "Ah, Peg, my dear, do you wish me to start pointing out some of the more outrageous Irish naming customs?" His Irish accent was suddenly very apparent; whether deliberate or not, Betsy couldn't tell.

Peg said, in a pure Midwestern accent, "Oh, Da, don't be such a dork!"

They all laughed.

Peg asked Betsy, "These Larson people, do they have children?"

"Yes, a girl, Emma Beth, who is three and a half and my goddaughter, and a little boy, Erik, who is nearly two."

The food came then and a silence fell while the trio dug in. After a few minutes, Peg said, "I hope you realize what you are doing to my attempts to convince my palate that pizza, hamburgers, and cafeteria food are all they serve in this part of the world."

"If I remember correctly," said Betsy, "it's all they serve on any campus."

"Then it's been going on since as far back as that?" asked Peg.

Betsy felt as if she'd been struck in the face.

Peg looked startled. "Did that come out of my wicked mouth, then?" she asked. "I'm so sorry!"

"It's all right," said Betsy. "I suppose it has been a long time."

"You're a nasty, evil girl and no child of mine," said Connor lightly, but with a hint of anger.

"I really am sorry, Da," said Peg. "I'll guard my tongue, I promise."

Looking back on the evening while lying in bed, Betsy reflected that Peg hadn't tried all that hard to keep her promise. There weren't any further digs, at least none as serious as that first one, but still, Betsy sensed that Peg had a problem with her. It seemed it was true that she saw Betsy as a threat. Betsy thought that strange in a woman of Peg's years. Normally only the very young were threatened by a new woman—oh. That was it. It wasn't that Betsy threatened the relationship between Peg and Connor, but the one between Connor and his first wife.

Not that there was one—there hadn't been for many years, even back before the divorce.

At least according to Connor.

But it was normal, even for adult children of divorce, to see a new relationship between Dad and a woman—or Mom and a man—as disloyal to the first spouse.

Many maintained a fiction that one or both of them pined for the lost spouse, perhaps even vowed to live a life of celibacy in honor of it, and the presence of a new love was a serious threat to that romantic nonsense.

And Peg's undergraduate degree was in art.

Oh, dear.

*   *   *

"REMEMBER *The Parent Trap?*" Betsy asked. "The version I remember starred Hayley Mills, but there was a more recent one. About twin girls separated as infants when their parents divorced, and how they found each other and concocted a plan to get their parents back together. A successful plan. The dream of every child of divorce, to get their parents back together."

"But Peg's not a child, for heaven's sake!" Connor said. "She's twenty-three years old! She knows the reasons for the divorce, and she's fine with it!"

"I will bet you ten dollars she has this vision of you brooding down your declining years, carrying a torch the size of Lady Liberty's for the one true love of your life."

"Rot!" he said.

"Then explain why she was rude to me."

"She wasn't rude."

"Of course she was. Tell me what she said to you on your way home from dinner last night."

"She said it was a delicious dinner in a beautiful restaurant overlooking a gorgeous view of Lake Minnetonka, which she thought was a silly name."

"About me, what did she say about me."

He hesitated. "She thought you were nice."

"I don't believe she said that. She said something rude, or at the most she said something defensible. You know, double meaning. Like I was pretty much as you described me—how did you describe me to her?"

His cheeks grew red, and she said, "I thought so."

"Now truly, *machree*, I think you're reading too much into this. She was a little nervous about meeting you, it's true, so I played down your sterling qualities so as not to scare her off entirely. But now she's met you, I'm sure she sees what a dear pet you are and will come to like you just as I do."

"I sure hope so. I don't want to cause trouble between the two of you."

"Of course you won't!"

"I'm not so sure. But I think she feels threatened, and it worries me."

"Ach, don't *fash* yourself," he said in an accent suddenly very Scottish—he could put on any British accent at the drop of a hat.

Normally it made her laugh, but not this time. Angrily, she turned away.

After supper she turned in early and wept into her pillow for half an hour.

"OH, dear," said Godwin in the shop the next morning. "All our little insecurities were on display, weren't they?"

"What's that supposed to mean?"

"I mean, you were so very sure he described you to his daughter in less than glowing terms."

"And I was right! Oh, I can just hear him: 'Not very tall, a little overweight, two ex-husbands,' the rat!"

Godwin came to take her hands in his. "My dear, dear, *dearest* boss, listen to yourself. He is wild about you, you know that. He wants his daughter to at least like you. Why would he say such unflattering things about you?"

Betsy turned away, blinking against tears.

Behind her, Godwin said in his gentlest voice, "Because you think he thinks that about you, right?"

Betsy sighed, "Oh, Goddy!" and a tear spilled over.

"And there you stand, a successful businesswoman with a sweet attitude—most of the time—and a generous heart. You think he doesn't know that? You think he wouldn't say something like that about you to his daughter? Look at you! You have big blue eyes and a curvy figure. You have a clever mind and a talent for solving criminal cases. You have loyal friends and employees. You're very pretty, almost beautiful, especially when you pay attention to your clothing. Your second ex-husband, when last seen, was eating his heart out because he let you get away. Am I making any impression at all on you?"

She turned back, eyes still shiny with tears, but of a wholly different kind. "Oh, Goddy!" He came and they shared a long hug.

"You make me feel like such a fool!"

"Good, I'm glad. Because you're behaving very foolishly."

"I'll invite him over for a home-cooked meal and we'll make up," Betsy said.

But Connor had a previous engagement with his daughter already set up for that evening and also said he was going to be busy for the next several days. He'd have to get back to Betsy about that supper sometime in the next week or two.

Betsy spent the next twenty-four hours switching from heartbreak to fury and back again, and nothing Godwin could say changed either mood.

She was in heartbreak mode when Jill Cross Larson came into the shop with something obviously on her mind.

"I'm here to pick up that pattern I asked you to pull for me," she announced.

Betsy reached into a desk drawer to lift out Paula Minkebige's Loon Lake, Number Seventeen in the Crossed Wing Collection.

Jill went on, "Plus I need some DMC floss." She headed for the cabinet of little drawers in which the floss lay sorted. "*And* I want to issue an invitation to you to come up and see what you have wrought for us. There's plenty to do, and the area is just beautiful. The cabin is going to be wonderful." She pulled a drawer open. "Besides," she added archly, "a little bird told me there is a person who needs to discover he misses you."

"Oh, I don't think I can get away right now . . ." Betsy sighed. She was trying to save money by working extra hours in the shop, thereby cutting back on her part-timers' hours. Employee pay was her biggest expense.

Jill, who had pulled a skein of 645, dark gray, and another of 924, dark blue-green, came over to the checkout desk to lean forward, her light blue eyes shining. "Think about it," she murmured. "Pine trees so tall their tops seem to tangle in the clouds, air cool and clean and a little sharp in the nose. Sky blue water in the lake, a deer half-seen in the woods, an eagle circling a clearing on still wings. A fire in the stove on a cool evening, a cup of cocoa, and pair of loons making that yearning, lonesome yodel down on the lake."

Against her will, Betsy's interest stirred. "You have loons?"

"Right down on our shore." She put the floss on the pattern, which was of a pair of adult loons, black-and-white-striped water birds. A fuzzy gray infant rode on one adult's back. "Like this, except it's August and the babies are grown now."

Betsy had never seen a loon in person, and had heard their eerie cries only in recordings. They had pointed beaks and heavy bones, she knew. They were very strange birds, the state bird of Minnesota.

She looked up into Jill's kind, concerned face and said, "When?"

"How about this weekend? Come for four days. Lars is taking Monday and Tuesday off because he's working all of Labor Day weekend. It'll be the first time we've brought the children up."

"Oh, I don't think—"

Godwin appeared from out of nowhere. "No, don't think. Just go. Consider this—what do you military folk call it? Emergency leave. Take emergency leave."

She looked at his face, also kind and concerned.

"All right," she said. She looked at Jill. "Yes, I'll come. Thank you."

Three

❖ ❖ ❖

THERE are two kinds of travel, goes an old saying: first class, and with children. The Larson children were well behaved, for nearly four and almost two—but they were lively little ones, and for them the three-hour drive to Thunder Lake was interminable. Lars stopped twice on the way up to turn them out of the SUV and let them run around. That worked for little Erik after the second time, when he fell asleep in his car seat. But Emma Beth, buckled into her car seat, couldn't find a DVD she liked, so she sang, loudly and off-key, the same three verses of "Old MacDonald," and asked after every other verse if they were there yet.

Jill and Lars discussed what they had done to the old cabin. It had been six weeks since they had taken possession. They had gone up on weekends to do some emergency repairs to make the place suitable for human habitation—which meant they had driven out the spiders, squirrels, mice, and mama raccoon that had taken up residence. They had unplugged the chimneys and propped up the miniature front porch. Lars had found and plugged a leak on the roof. There was no electricity pending an inspection of the wiring by a professional, and the only source of water was a hand pump outside the cabin.

Betsy, no fan of roughing it, was prepared to put up with a certain amount of primitive living for the sake of getting really far away—cell phones didn't work on that side of the lake, and the Larsons didn't plan to install a landline, at least not right away.

But thoughts of a fugitive spider or two nesting in her hair overnight and no hot shower in the morning were discouraging.

At last they turned off the highway onto a secondary road lined with immense pine trees set here and there with aspen. They turned off that onto a gravel road even more closely set with huge pines, and off that onto a dirt road, and off that onto a lane that was two barely visible tire tracks. It led up a steep little rise and into a small clearing—and on the far edge of the clearing stood a little log cabin.

"Are we here yet?" asked Emma Beth.

"Yes, darling, we're here."

"Yaaaaaaay," said Emma Beth. "Look, Godmama, we're here! Wake up, Airey, we're here! Airey, Airey, wake up!" She reached over and pushed Betsy into the side of Erik's car seat.

Erik, startled, began that thin wailing of a baby awakened against his will.

"Are we going to have that kind of weekend?" asked Lars in a very heavy voice.

"No, Daddy," said Emma Beth humbly.

"Good."

"I'm sorry."

"Very good." Lars shut off the engine and climbed out. His open door admitted a heavy fragrance of pine.

He opened the door on Emma Beth's side and unbuckled her seat belt. He lifted her out and then suddenly up and around, high in the air. She shrieked with laughter.

Betsy slid out on the same side and stood for a few moments, enjoying the sunshine and clean, sharp-scented air.

Meanwhile Jill opened the door and unbuckled Erik from his car seat. "Ma-*ma*!" he wailed, and she lifted him into her arms.

"There, there, baby," she soothed, and he quickly fell silent while he looked around with wet, wondering eyes.

Emma Beth, put down, turned slowly to look up at an enormous pine going up, in her eyes, forever. "Oh my goo'ness!" she murmured. "Oh my goo'ness, is this tree ours?"

"Yes, darling," said Jill with laughter in her voice.

Lars said complacently, "All these trees are ours."

But what Betsy was looking at was the pretty little cabin across the clearing. A for-real log cabin, with a low-pitched roof and a tiny porch. An old-fashioned long-handled pump was near the left corner, standing on a circle of gray planks. The cabin was right on the edge of a drop-off, down which marched more trees. She walked toward them, past the cabin, for a look downward, and saw a very crooked path—a series of uneven switchbacks really—that led down among brush and pine trees to the shore of a lake. She couldn't see more than a twinkle of water because of the foliage. Some kind of bird was calling in a monotonous high-pitched skree, and a squirrel scolded nearby.

"Betsy?" called Jill.

"Coming!" She turned and went back around to the front of the cabin, where Jill and Lars stood. The children watched curiously from the patchy lawn behind them as their mother made strange ducking and waving motions. As Betsy got closer, she could see why: spider webs, some with spiders on them.

"Honestly, you'd never think I cleared the spiders off just last weekend!" exclaimed Jill, waving her arms. Betsy admired her nerve; if she had encountered a set of spider webs, she'd have retreated to the car until someone else cleared the porch of them.

The porch was a small concrete slab about the size of a city sidewalk square, set with two slender pillars holding up a tiny peaked roof. Two long boards leaned against the outsides of the pillars, helping them support the roof. The concrete slab sloped forward just a little from the front door, making Betsy wonder about the stability of the soil under the cabin. But surely, over a century, the porch would be tilted farther down than that if the soil were really unstable.

"Ahhhh," sighed Jill at last, dusting her hands and brushing at the long sleeves of her shirt, satisfied that the porch was clear. There were still a few webs stretched between the roof of the porch and the debarked logs of the cabin's front wall.

Lars opened the sagging screen door and unlocked the gray wooden door behind it. He had to push hard—and he was a big, strong man—before the door opened with a groan.

Emma Beth came close behind her father and mother into the cabin, Betsy bringing up the rear holding Erik's wee little hand.

The house appeared dark after the bright sunlight of the clearing, and they all stood a few moments to allow their eyes time to adjust.

They stood at one end of an open room twenty-four feet front to back. The walls were chinked logs and the ceiling ran up past the rafters to the boards of the roof. There was badly worn pink linoleum in the dining area and a flattened, elderly, gray-blue carpet on the living room area. The windows were small, about four feet above the floor, and twice as wide as they were high.

The adults and children were standing in the dining area furnished with an elderly card table and three folding chairs. The air was warm but musty—Lars went to pull open a window.

A pot-bellied stove squatted on a metal plate that crossed the border between the dining and living areas. Beyond it were a sofa and chair made of yellow logs, each with folded dark blue blankets and sleeping bags in lieu of cushions.

A small, seriously out-of-date kitchen was on their right— the stove actually appeared to be the sort that burned wood, and the refrigerator was an old-fashioned ice box—which explained the two large bags of ice cubes in the rearmost part of the SUV. There was a windowed back door on the far wall leading to a back porch. The place was shabby but orderly.

"*Nice!*" pronounced Erik cheerfully. Though not yet two, he had a budding vocabulary.

"Are we going to sleep here?" asked Emma, not happily.

"Yes, darling. You and Erik get the bedroom; Mama and Daddy will sleep on the back porch."

"Where is the bedroom?" asked Emma.

"Over here." Jill led the way to the farther of two doors, which opened into a room about twelve by twelve. It had a full-size bed with a foam-rubber mattress. "We threw the old mattress out," she said to Betsy. "The mice had made an apartment building of it."

Emma laughed. "Apar'ment building for the mice!"

There was an ancient, dark brown wicker chest of drawers, a matching wicker bookcase, and a wicker nightstand. A battery lantern, the kind with a hard plastic shade, was on the nightstand.

"You'll each get your sleeping bag and you'll sleep side by side, comfortable as two bugs in a rug."

"Bug!" shouted Erik joyously. "Bug!" He made a wet buzzing noise and laughed.

"Will we hear the loons tonight?" asked Betsy.

Emma said anxiously, "No, no, they aren't here."

"Yes, they are," said Jill firmly. She added, to Betsy, "She's heard them on camping trips and is afraid of them."

Lars said, "If you hear them and they scare you, you come and tell me."

"If I cry, you will make them go away!" said Emma Beth, pleased.

"No, for two reasons. Can you guess what they are?"

Emma Beth shook her head.

"First, because they can't hurt you. In fact, they are very shy and afraid of people. They're just birds, about the size of ducks. You aren't afraid of ducks, are you?"

Emma shook her head, smiling at the notion that she'd be afraid of a duck.

"Second, because this is their home. You wouldn't like it if someone bigger than us came and chased us out of our house, would you?"

"You wouldn't let them!"

"Well, if they were bigger than me—"

"Nobody's bigger than you, Daddy!"

Lars laughed. He was six feet, six inches tall and proportionately broad, a blond Viking with narrow, sea gray eyes, and perhaps a touch too much jaw. "That's mostly true, I guess. But people here have agreed to share the lake with the loons and the ducks and the turtles. And what does that mean about the loons?"

Emma conceded, "We don't bother them. But they bother us!"

"No, they bother *you*. *I* like them."

Emma turned to her mother with a pleading face. "No, honey face," said Jill, "I like them, too."

"Nice!" contributed Erik, unsolicited.

So Emma turned to her godmother. "Do you like loons?"

Betsy said, "I don't know. I want to sit up tonight and listen for them. Then I'll tell you."

Jill said, "I think that's a good idea. Now come on, I'll show you the rest of the place and tell you our plans for it."

The bathroom had been furnished in the fifties with a secondhand pedestal sink and a toilet with an overhead tank—which actually put them right back in style. Without electricity to operate a pump, there was no water. Lars tried the toilet, which obediently flushed. But the bucket on the floor clearly indicated where the water for a repeat performance came from.

"That old-fashioned pump out in the yard is currently the sole source for all our water," said Lars. "It's good water, doesn't taste of iron like a lot of water up here."

Jill said, "We'll have electricity soon, and we'll install a hot water heater and a new kitchen stove operating off a propane tank, which we'll also install."

Lars said, "The water pump is in, it just needs electricity to make it work."

Jill smiled. "I want to replace that tub with a shower. Wait till I show you the catalog photo of the tile I want to use in here. Meanwhile, this weekend I think we should get rid of the carpet."

"It is kind of musty in here," said Lars. He stepped back into the bedroom to open the window over the bed. Like those in the rest of the cabin, it was double paned to swing inward from the middle, and screened on the outside. A welcome pine-scented breeze drifted in.

The back porch ran the width of the cabin and had large windows. Amazingly, the screens were intact, if rusty, which was great because the windows were unglazed. The porch was furnished with a daybed, settee, chair, and rocker, all made of small yellow logs.

"These were all covered with quilts," noted Jill. "Ancient, faded, moldy quilts."

"Oh, too bad!" said Betsy. "I love old quilts."

"Mama said the mice weed on them," said Emma Beth in a low, scandalized voice.

"Yes, they did," said Jill. "And chewed them just about

to ribbons. We had to throw them away with the mattress. But look here." In a metal-clad chest under a window were more quilts. Protected from rain and sun, all they needed was a good airing.

"I'm going to go get the ice put away," said Lars, "and start bringing in the luggage."

The top quilt, a twin size, was a double wedding ring pattern, worked in still-bright shades of red, purple, green, and blue. "You can sleep under this tonight," said Jill to Betsy. The one under it was full size, in a pattern called log cabin, made of blocks of narrow brown, gray, and tan strips, each block having a traditional red square in its center. Very likely the quilter made this one especially for the cabin, thought Betsy. And under that—"Hey, where are the children?" asked Jill, missing their chatter.

As if in reply, there came a loud, high-pitched scream from outside.

Four

BEFORE Jill could get to the back door, Lars came rushing through from inside the cabin. Betsy turned to look out one of the big screened windows, with Jill suddenly beside her.

The screamer was Emma Beth. She was standing on the top of the switchback path leading down the steep hill, making a sound like an overheated teakettle. And rolling away from her down the trail was Airey, his red hair flashing in the broken sunlight, emitting a thin, uneven wail.

Lars ran after him in a series of huge plunges. Emma Beth's shrill cries cut off when she saw her father in action. He leaped over his son as he neared him. As he slid to a backward stop, Airey rolled onto his boot tops. Lars swooped him up. The baby shed dead leaves, pine needles, and bits of weed as Lars held him dangling at arm's length, but after a moment's shocked silence Airey said uncertainly, "Nice?"

Lars laughed his big laugh and hugged the boy. "Very nice!" he declared. Then he looked him over for injuries, finding nothing but a few scratches. "You were very brave, Airey," he declared. "But don't go outside again unless we come, too, okay?"

"'Kay?" echoed the uncomprehending toddler.

"And you, young lady," Lars added in an entirely different tone, starting back for the top.

Emma Beth said hastily, "I din't know he'd fall. We just wanted to see the lady. I thought she was a bear but she was a lady."

Jill said from the doorway, "If you look out and see a bear, you'd better stay in the cabin. Don't go near it. Bears think little children are delicious."

Emma Beth disagreed, shaking her head. "No, no, if you are a good girl, you can pet a bear."

"Only with a hand you don't want anymore," said Lars, reaching the top and touching his daughter on her fair head. The touch was gentle, but his expression was very firm.

Emma Beth looked up at him, her eyes gone large and round. "He would bite my hand off?"

"Truly. And then your ears, and then your nose. Bears around here aren't tame and they aren't nice." He looked hard at his son. "Bears are not nice," he repeated.

"No' nice," said Airey. "No' nice," he repeated to his sister in a firm voice.

"Oh-kay," said Emma Beth, discouraged. She brightened. "But it wasn't a bear, it was a lady."

"Where did you see a lady?" asked Lars.

"Over there, in the middle of the trees." Emma Beth pointed to a place at the top of the steep hill where the trees were thickly clustered.

"What did she look like, darling?" asked Jill.

"I don't know. She was just a lady. She had on brown so I thought she was a bear. I couldn't see her very good."

"See her very well," corrected Jill.

"See her very well," repeated Emma Beth obediently.

"Did she say anything, or wave?"

"No, she saw me seeing her and went away."

"Did she run away?"

Emma Beth thought. "No, she just walked away. I thought she was a bear. Mama, are all bears naughty?"

With her eyes, Jill was searching the area Emma Beth had indicated, looking for the brown lady. She said, "I'm sure the bears don't think they are being naughty. They're just hungry."

Emma Beth looked around, drawing up her little shoulders. "Maybe we should go home now."

Lars laughed. "No, it's all right with the animals if we come for a visit. But don't touch. And if you want to go out for a walk, you must bring Mama or Daddy with you, all right? Or you might get lost, or see a bear and accidentally bother him, and he wouldn't like that."

"Bears won't eat mamas or daddies," concluded Emma Beth.

"That's right. Now, how about I set up the grill and cook some hot dogs for you and Airey?"

Later, over grilled hot dogs and potato salad—they'd

found a crumbling picnic table in the shed on an earlier visit and dragged it out now—Betsy asked, "Why Airey? Why not Ricky?"

"Emma Beth started calling him Airey," said Jill, "and like a lot of fond, doting parents, we thought it was so cute we imitated her. And now it's stuck. Of course he knows his full name, Erik Sigurd Larson, after his two grandfathers, because that's what I call him when he's misbehaving."

Betsy nodded, feeling grateful on behalf of the toddler that at least one grandfather had a name that could pass muster in any company. Knut and Bjorn were not uncommon names among old-fashioned Norwegians, nor was Swan. Somehow Betsy did not think Erik—Airey—would thank his parents for naming him Airey Swan.

All the leftovers were scrupulously gathered into a plastic bag, which would be taken away when they left. "People around here have some strict rules about it," said Lars. "No one wants the bears to learn that humans are a source of food."

"Bears like hot dogs better than noses," declared Emma Beth.

"It's possible they do," said Lars, nodding.

"Nose!" Airey said, pointing at his own tiny appendage, and broke into loud laughter.

After lunch they all took the path of steep switchbacks down to the lakeshore. About halfway down, Emma Beth said to Betsy, "That's the biggest tree I ever saw," and pointed to an enormous white pine.

"Wow, that is big," said Betsy, looking up and searching futilely for the top branches, hidden beyond the tops of the other trees.

Emma Beth and Airey preceded their parents on a detour to the base of the tree. Emma Beth tried to hug it, but her little arms could not reach even a quarter of the way around. Betsy came to help, but it was only when Jill and Airey joined in that they managed, barely, to encircle the tree with their arms.

Betsy became aware that a "kree, kree, kree" bird sound she'd been hearing for a while seemed to be coming from the top of this giant.

"Do you know what kind of bird is calling?" she asked.

"It's a bald eagle," said Jill. "Didn't I tell you? We have our very own bald eagle family nesting in the top of this tree. This is their fifth year, according to the locals. Last year they raised two youngsters, this year only one. That's him calling. He's fully fledged, and it's time for him to make his first flight, so his parents have stopped feeding him."

"You have your very own bald eagle family? This place of yours just gets cooler and cooler! Where are his parents? Did they abandon him?"

"No, they're around here somewhere, keeping watch."

As if to illustrate, a descending "skreeee" sounded from down near the bottom of the hill, a sound made familiar from television.

The youngster, encouraged by the reply, called again and again, but all he got was an occasional reply from the adults.

Airey stooped and picked up a small, dark brown feather from amid a low heap of dead leaves. He looked it over thoughtfully while a sentence formed in his head. "Baby bird," he said at last, holding it out to his mother.

"You know, I think you're right, I think this did belong

to the baby up in the nest," said Jill. "But we can't keep it, it's an eagle feather and we are not allowed to have an eagle feather. Put it back—and find something else."

Airey made a disappointed face, but put the feather back exactly where he had found it, and instead picked up a tiny, long-needled twig of pine. He held it out for inspection, and his mother approved, so he pushed it into a pocket of his overalls.

They returned to the switchback trail and continued to the lakeshore. There was no sandy beach, but a grassy clearing that stood about a foot above the level of the water. Grass hung over in a fringe whose edges just touched the tops of the little waves that lapped the shore. There was a smoke-blackened fire pit near where an adolescent aspen leaned steeply out over the water.

"We're going to lose that tree," predicted Lars. "Next heavy rainstorm it'll fall in."

"Poor thing," said Betsy. She stood on the bank and looked out over the lake. There was a round island about eighty yards out with a fallen-down cabin sitting among big trees near the shore. Betsy had looked at a map of Cass County before coming on this trip and been amused to notice that the lake was shaped like a duckling mostly. That is, the back end was a confusion of marsh and ponds without a clearly defined tail and feet, but the long body and one stubby wing were clear and the head had a perfectly shaped bill. Even the island was properly placed to be an eye.

"Why isn't this lake called Duck Lake?" she asked now.

Jill said, "Because every now and then it gives out a sound like thunder. No one knows why. The sound seems to come from the deepest part of the lake, which is just a little down from where we are. It's spring fed, and the movement of water may cause earth on the bottom to shift and rocks to fall or grind. It doesn't do it very often or predictably, so no one's been able to witness it happening down there. But it happens often enough to earn the name *Thunder Lake*."

"Is that little house ours, too?" asked Emma Beth, pointing at a miniature log building on the Larson property just up from where they were standing.

"Yes, it's a boat house," said Lars. "When we come next year, we will put a boat in there."

"Can we go for a boat ride?" asked Emma Beth.

The Larsons had brought an inflatable rowboat with them.

"Maybe tomorrow," said Lars. "I want to get up on the roof today and see how my patch is holding up."

"And I want to explore the shed," said Jill, "to see if we can convert it into a garage. And start taking up the carpet. But we can come back down here tonight and build a campfire if you like. Make s'mores."

"Yayyyyy!" cheered Emma Beth, doing a little dance. She had enjoyed them at a backyard barbecue earlier in the summer.

"Aaaaaaay!" echoed Airey, waving his arms. He was not sure of the reason, but pleased to join the fun.

"Do you have any neighbors around here?" asked Betsy as they started the trip back up the slope.

Lars said, "About half a mile down the shore there's another cabin exactly like this one, or near enough, owned by a bachelor fisherman. The man who built ours made a career out of building log cabins for summer visitors; there are six or eight of them on lakes in the area. In the other direction, about a quarter mile from here, we have a young couple. He's a dentist and she's a pharmacist. But instead of a cabin, they have a modern house, though they use it just in the summer. The next cabin is more than a mile away, but we hear more are to be built next year, if the market recovery holds up. There are only a dozen cabins currently on Thunder Lake."

Jill said, "Maybe the pharmacist is the woman in brown that Emma Beth thought was a bear. But if so, it's funny she didn't come over to say hello."

"Does anyone live on the island?" Betsy turned to look back at the water. She had seen only the tumbledown ruin on the island, but maybe there was a house on the other side. She had seen a clapboard cabin and a fine, big house near the shore on the other side of the lake. The many trees hid other dwellings over there. And now the big trees on this side again hid everything but glimpses of the glittering water.

"Not right now," said Lars. "There's a lodge across the lake, down toward the foot, and rumors they're going to build another one up at our end. The existing lodge rents fishing boats. I'm surprised we didn't see any on the lake—you can tell them by their daylight yellow color."

"Where are the loons?" asked Betsy.

"They're out there, fishing. But they're hard to see unless two males get into a territorial battle. They only call at night. We don't go looking for them because if they're disturbed, they'll relocate."

Later, while the children napped on the back porch, Jill, Betsy, and Lars took on the awful task of lifting the ancient, moldy carpet. Lars used a box cutter to free it around the edges of the living room and bedroom, and Jill and Betsy pulled it up. Lars cut it into manageable pieces, Betsy rolled it up, and Jill dragged it outside. She came back in from one journey to report that it was starting to look like rain.

Under the carpet were two layers of linoleum, the top one matching the pale pink of the dining area. Lars, cutting deep with the box cutter, went through both layers and, curious, pried up a corner.

"Say, Jill, take a look at this!" he called.

Under the two layers of linoleum were wide planks of varnished wood. Betsy came for a look as well, and watched while Lars pulled up a bigger piece of cracked, faded linoleum and the less-faded brown-and-green piece under it. Pieces of linoleum stuck to the planks, but enough was clear for Jill to make an exclamation of delight.

"Do you see that?" she demanded of Betsy.

"Yes, a wooden floor. Is it hardwood?"

"It's old-growth pine, I'm sure of it. See how fine the grain is? What do you think, Lars? Am I right, old-growth?"

"I think so," he said with a happy smile. "Imagine covering this up with linoleum!"

"Maybe it's a mess in the middle," said Jill.

"Then we'll refinish it," vowed Lars. "Man, look how broad those planks are. I wonder if they were sawn from a tree on the property. I'm pretty sure the walls were built of trees cut down right here."

Betsy thought of the old tree on the downward slope to the lake. "I'm glad the loggers left one for the eagles to use," she said.

"Say," said Jill thoughtfully, "suppose we pay for the renovations to this place with that tree. How many board feet do you think that big old pine would make?" she asked Lars.

He sat back on his heels to consider the question.

Betsy said, "Oh, Jill, you *wouldn't*!"

Jill began to laugh. "No, of course we wouldn't. What's more, we can't."

"Why not?"

"Because we signed a scenic easement agreement with the Department of Natural Resources that we wouldn't cut down any trees or alter the lakeshore or put up any new buildings. In return, they pay us a sum that's about equal to one mortgage payment a year."

The removal of the linoleum continued. Though it was early afternoon, the sky darkened outside, and there came a faint rumble of thunder. Jill went into the kitchen and brought back three kerosene lanterns with tall, clear-glass chimneys. She lit them with the long-necked lighter Lars had used to start the charcoal burning in the grill. Their mellow, golden glow filled the room, making it cozy against the storm brewing outdoors.

Suddenly a loud crack of lightning lit up the windows and a strong gust of wind blew in through the screens.

"Mama?" came a sleepy query from the porch. Thunder rolled loudly across the clearing. *"Mama!"*

"Mama!" said another, younger voice, this one full of tears.

Lars and Jill went out on the porch to comfort and reassure their frightened children.

"Who's afraid of a little old thunder?" asked Lars in an amused, scoffing voice.

"Not me," declared Emma Beth, wiping her cheeks with both palms. "Silly old thunder!"

"T'under nice!" said Airey in unconvinced tones. His voice was still choked with tears. "Want Bin-kee-kee-kee," he said, surrendering to his sobs, then trying to muffle them on his mother's shoulder.

"Why, of course you do," said Jill. "Here, come with me and we'll find Binky."

Binky, Betsy knew, was a blue teddy bear who had been Airey's companion since he was born. Jill went into the bedroom and in a few seconds the two returned, Binky safe in his small master's arms. Poor Binky had been kicked, sat on, slept on, dragged through mud puddles, shoved across playground equipment, and run through the washer and dryer almost as often as he had been hugged and kissed in his short life. And he looked it. His head lolled dangerously to one side, his eyes didn't match, and his nose had been rubbed completely off. But Airey loved him passionately, and wiped the last of his tears away on the bear's face.

Airey was put into the log easy chair with Binky—the chair had been moved into the dining area of the big room. After closing all the windows, Jill and Lars moved the cushions from the porch furniture into the bedroom, and operations on the carpet resumed. Emma Beth "helped" by holding one end of the hunks of carpet while Betsy rolled them up.

"Well, look at this!" said Jill after a little while. She was in the center of the carpeted area.

"What, you found the damaged part of the floor?" asked Lars, not looking around.

"No, look, there's a trapdoor."

"There is? Where?"

"Here, in the middle of the floor." Lars and Betsy came for a look. Jill had pulled up random pieces of linoleum, looking for the damaged boards. Instead, she had found this.

The trapdoor was about half uncovered and the three of them quickly pulled back more linoleum to reveal the rest of it.

The door was made from the same boards as the rest of the floor, set in so it was flush. Even the handle was inset, with a small piece of wood filling the space where fingers could be inserted to grasp and lift.

"I didn't know there was a basement to this place," said Lars.

"It wasn't mentioned in the legal description," said Betsy.

"It can't be a regular basement," said Jill. "There are no windows on the outside to bring light into it."

"That's right," said Lars, half closing his eyes and nodding as he walked in memory around the cabin.

"Well, are you going for a look or not?" demanded Betsy, eaten up with curiosity.

"Lars, bring me a flashlight, please," said Jill.

"Sure." He headed for the kitchen and began opening cabinets and drawers in a search. "Here it is." He came back. "You found it, you get to go down first."

Jill, meanwhile, had picked out the fragment of wood, which had been cut and smoothed to fit the opening, and lifted the door. It opened with a very traditional squeal-creak, and its edges were draped with the traditional cobwebs.

Betsy could see a set of rough wood steps leading down into darkness.

"I bet it's full of old clothes and shoes," Lars said. "Since this place doesn't have an attic."

Jill turned on the flashlight and went down the steps. In a few seconds her voice was heard. "Betsy, take the children into the bedroom, will you please? Lars, come take a look." Her voice was brisk and a trifle stiff.

"What is it, what have you found?" asked Betsy.

"I'll tell you in a little while. Just take the children into the bedroom. And close the door."

Five

❖ ❖ ❖

Less than a minute later, Betsy, from inside the bedroom, heard the Larson's SUV start up and drive off. Jill came into the bedroom right after that, with a look on her face that Betsy interpreted as world-weary.

"What is it, what did you find?" Betsy asked.

"An S-K-E-L-E-T-O-N," Jill spelled out.

"No!"

"What's a ess-kay, Mama?" asked Emma Beth from the center of the bed where she sat straight-legged. Airey lay curled up beside her with Binky.

"It means some old bones, Baby," said Jill.

"I'm not a baby, Airey is a baby," replied the child.

"That's true, you aren't a baby anymore. So what shall I call you? How about 'child'?"

"Em-Beth. I like Em-Beth. It's Emma Beth, only shorter." She sounded as if she'd been thinking about it for some while.

"All right, for the rest of today you are Em-Beth. Now, Daddy's gone to use the telephone at The Lone Wolf General Store. He's going to call some people who are going to come and look at the old bones." Jill looked at Betsy. "It's a root cellar, dirt walls and floor. Takes up maybe a third of the area of the upstairs. There are some shelves down there with some old home-canned goods on them."

"How old is the—I mean, how old are the bones?"

"They look very old. It's naked, no clothing visible."

"Mama, you said naked!" said Emma Beth in a shocked voice.

"You're right, Em-Beth, I shouldn't have said that word in front of company. Little pitchers have big ears, my grandmother used to say whenever the conversation got interesting and we were in the room."

Betsy laughed softly. "My grandmother said the same thing. Then we got sent out to play."

"Us, too. We'll have to make different arrangements now, because it's raining."

It was a sparse rain with no wind, but the occasional flicker of lightning and the lengthy pause before the rumble of thunder meant this was just the leading edge of the storm. The sky was very dark.

"Looks like it's going to come down in buckets pretty soon," said Jill.

"Jill, may I go look at the bones?" Betsy was not fond of gory stuff, but a skeleton wasn't gory.

Jill hesitated, then said, "If you'll stay on the steps. I don't want the scene disturbed." She handed Betsy the flashlight.

The cellar wasn't very deep, barely head-high—and Betsy was five feet, four inches tall. The steps down into it were made of thick planks of unfinished wood, gray with age. Betsy stood on the bottom one, shoulders hunched to keep her hair from brushing one of the cobwebby timbers supporting the ceiling.

Two of the walls were lined with a double row of thick, rough-plank shelves, supported by pegs hammered into the dirt. There were perhaps a dozen glass jars, very dusty, with some long, greenish vegetables suspended in them, probably green beans. What had probably once been white adhesive tape with a short message—a date?—could be discerned on the closest jar. Like the ceiling, the shelves were draped with cobwebs.

Betsy let the flashlight linger on the shelves for a few long seconds before bracing herself and turning it downward.

The skeleton lay in a disarticulated heap in the center of the floor. Its details were blurred with dust but it seemed all there. The skull was turned upward and away from the rest of the bones, its square eyeholes looking toward her, a gold molar gleaming faintly under the flashlight's beam. The rib cage had collapsed, the lower jaw lay teeth down among them. The shinbones were across the thighbones—Betsy had the sudden thought that the body had initially lain with its knees drawn up. One arm was outflung, the ends of the fingers mere suggestive bumps under the dust.

There were no footprints; obviously Jill had stayed on the steps, too.

There were small round objects here and there around the skeleton, barely discernable, and Betsy puzzled over them for a while. Then, *Oh*, she thought, *buttons.* But there did not seem to be any remnant of clothing present. That was another puzzlement until—*Mice*, thought Betsy, recalling the fate of the mattress and quilts. She shuddered at the thought of mice making nests from a dead man's clothes.

But was it a man? It could be a woman. Betsy didn't know how to tell the sex of a skeleton.

Who are you? She thought at the skeleton. *And how did you come to be here in this root cellar?*

There came no reply. She went back up the steps.

Jill was sitting cross-legged on the bed regaling the children with the story of Jack and the Beanstalk.

Lars got back a few minutes later, ahead of the heavy rain, but only just, rushing back into the cabin right as the wind picked up. Betsy went out to greet him. He had a big block of something wrapped in newspaper.

"Ice for the ice box," he explained and went to put it in a compartment at the top of the refrigerator, next to a much-diminished bag of ice cubes. "Sheriff's on his way," he added.

"Deputy John!" cried Emma Beth happily from her place in the bedroom doorway.

"No, honey; up here they have a different deputy. I don't know his name yet."

"Will he want a Cherry Coke?" In Emma Beth's experience, a deputy always appreciated a Cherry Coke.

"We can ask him when he comes. But first we'll have to talk some business over with him. I want you and Airey to stay in the bedroom while we talk. Can you do that?" Lars could put on an air of authority that was scary. He wore it lightly now, but it was unmistakable, and Emma Beth nodded. Even Airey nodded, his face solemn.

"Yes, Daddy. Can Mama stay with us?"

"No, darling, Mama has to talk business, too."

"I can stay with you," said Betsy. "We can color and I can read to you."

"Color!" cheered Emma Beth.

"Book!" said Airey.

"We'll do both," decided Betsy.

The children were each given a cookie and a glass of milk to entertain them until the sheriff's department arrived. When it did, it came in the person of a stocky Native American man. He drove a white patrol car with big green letters spelling SHERIFF on its side. He wore the brown and tan sheriff's department uniform under a yellow rain slicker, and a shower cap over his hat. He introduced himself as Deputy Jack McElroy—pronounced "mackle-roy"—and stood streaming water onto the linoleum floor right inside the door while Lars introduced himself as a sergeant on the Excelsior police department and produced identification to confirm it. McElroy's eyebrows lifted and Betsy thought she could detect a slight lessening of the tension he had brought into the cabin.

"This is my wife, Jill, our children Emma Beth and Erik, and this is our friend Betsy Devonshire, also of Excelsior. We bought this cabin six weeks ago, and this is our fourth visit to it. We were taking up the floor coverings when Jill discovered the trapdoor." He turned and gestured at the yawning opening.

McElroy took off his hat and slicker while Jill swiftly explained how they had made the discovery.

"We only looked and didn't disturb the scene," Jill concluded.

"All right, Em-Beth and Airey, you come with me," said Betsy. "We'll get you out of the way so this man can look at things and talk to your mama and daddy."

"Thank you," said McElroy, nodding at her, as he pulled a big, black Kell flashlight from his utility belt. He had draped the slicker over one of the folding chairs.

He walked to the open trapdoor and shone the light down the steps. Then he bent himself into a shape suitable to go down and slowly sank out of sight. Betsy, herding the children into the bedroom, heard him give a low whistle. Then she firmly closed the door and said, "Let's color!"

Soon there was the sound of other arrivals, men's feet clumping around, a woman's voice—not Jill's—and voices giving orders. It went on and on and on; the children were getting bored and cranky long before the door opened and Betsy changed places with Jill.

Betsy was so relieved when Jill came in that it was a shock to find herself confronted by the grim face of a man in civilian attire. He stood in the dining area looking at her. "Good afternoon," he said in a voice oddly light for his size and expression. "You are Elizabeth Devonshire?"

"Yessir," replied Betsy.

"I'm Investigator Mix, with the Bureau of Criminal Apprehension. Will you sit down over here?" She joined him at the table, sitting on the least wobbly folding chair. Betsy could hear men's voices—no, one was a woman's—down in the cellar, speaking so quietly she couldn't understand the words.

Mix said, "We're here assisting the Cass County Sheriff's Department in this matter. Is it all right if I ask you some questions?"

"Certainly. Ask whatever you like."

"How long have you known the Larsons?"

"I've known Jill since before she was married, since before I inherited my needlework shop." Betsy told him how she had come to Minnesota some years back. Guided by his questions, she explained about the other company she owned, New York Motto, and how it had led to Jill and Lars buying the cabin.

"You bought it sight unseen?" Mix asked.

"Yes, I almost never visit the property New York Motto buys. I'm a silent partner in the business and pretty much stay out of the day-to-day running of it. But this time I did take an interest, directing my partner to look for cabins in the northern area of the state, on or near a lake. Jill and Lars looked at several and said this cabin was what they wanted, so I recommended the purchase and sale."

"Have you done something like that before?"

"No, most of the people I know don't know about New York Motto, or if they do, they aren't interested in my help acquiring property. This was a special case."

Satisfied that there was no link between Betsy and the skeleton, he thanked her and was about to dismiss her when she asked, "Do we have to stay here until you're finished?

The kids are getting bored, and frankly I'm tired of sitting in that room myself."

Mix smiled and said, "I understand. And I think we're done with you. Unfortunately, we're not done with processing the scene."

Betsy's heart sank until he continued, "Is there someplace nearby you could go? There are motels and resorts in the area, if you're willing to stay until we've finished up here."

"How long might that be?"

"I'd say we'll finish up by late tonight or early tomorrow."

Betsy turned in her chair and called, "Lars? Can you come here a minute?"

He came in off the back porch with an inquiring look on his face. "Something wrong?"

"No, in fact you might be pleased to know that Investigator Mix says we can find someplace else to stay for the night while they work on the scene. I don't know about you, but the children and I have a case of cabin fever."

Lars chuckled. "Me, too. Just sitting around is hard on all of us. All right, let me talk with Jill."

Jill came out of the bedroom, leaving behind the sounds of whining children, to gratefully accept the offer of escape.

The three adults swiftly packed two suitcases and an overnight bag, exchanged cell phone numbers with Investigator Mix, and departed.

They went up the road in the rain to The Lone Wolf and used their landline phone. Anderson's, the resort on Thunder Lake, had no vacancies. A motel outside of Remer was full. Two resorts on the way to Longville had no cabins available.

Longville itself had a motel, but it was also full. However, a place called Camp O' My Dreams just the other side of Longville had two bed-and-breakfast rooms available, one with two beds, the other with a single queen-size bed.

"We'll take both rooms," declared Jill and Betsy in one voice.

The rooms were in the finished basement of a new, large, and severely plain house overlooking Long Lake. The shoreline was occupied by four RVs and one mobile home near the house, and six cabins of varying sizes and styles farther down. Mature trees dotted the landscape, and the view down the length of the lake was lovely.

"Will you want breakfast in the morning?" asked Wilma Griffin, the middle-aged widow who owned the property.

"Yes, please," said Lars.

He and the children took the room with two beds, while Jill and Betsy took the other. The rooms were simply furnished, but clean, and the mattresses on the beds seemed comfortable.

Betsy treated everyone to dinner at the nicest restaurant in Longville, Patrick's, which had an extensive menu and a big salad bar. The children had "busketti" while the adults ordered the walleye—listed, to Betsy's amusement, under "Seafood."

Driving back on the rain-wet street toward the main street of the little town, Emma Beth suddenly shouted, "A turtle, a turtle!" and Lars, thinking one of the creatures was trying to cross the road, slammed on his brakes.

But Emma Beth had spied a bronze statue of a turtle on a pedestal between the street and the sidewalk. Hanging from a nearby building was a big sign declaring LONGVILLE THE

TURTLE RACING CAPITOL OF MINNESOTA and advertising Tuesday afternoon turtle races.

"Can turtles run?" asked Emma Beth. "Can we watch? When is Tuesday?"

"Day after tomorrow is Tuesday," admitted Jill. "And we'll see."

"See tuttle!" declared Airey, to seal the deal.

Six

COMING upstairs to the table the next morning, Jill was pleased to see that breakfast was ample: pancakes, fruit in sweetened juice, oatmeal, sausage patties, toast, orange juice, milk, coffee. Wilma sat at the table with them, along with an older couple who had come every year for the past dozen years. The fourth room had been taken by a pair of fishermen, who skipped breakfast to get out on the water at first light, which came around five at this time of year.

Talk was of the pleasures of Cass County, fishing and hiking, of the nearness of Lake Itasca, source of the Mississippi River, where it was so narrow it could be crossed on stepping-stones.

Toward the end of the meal, searching for something further to talk about, Wilma asked what brought the quintet to her camp.

"We're not talking about it in front of the children," said Jill, speaking in her best neutral voice.

"Oh, you're getting a D-I-V-O-R-C-E," spelled the female member of the older couple.

"No, that's not it at all," said Lars with a laugh. He finished his third cup of coffee in a single big gulp. "We came up here to work on a cabin we've just bought over on Thunder Lake, and found something in the cellar that made us decide to move out for a day while it gets cleaned up."

Jill thought that too good a hint and would have changed the subject to how good the pancakes were, but Emma Beth spoke up.

"A deputy sheriff came to see us," announced the child, making Jill's mouth twitch with exasperation. "He's nice but he's not Deputy John, he's a different deputy."

"Oh, my God, you're the people who found a—"

Jill dropped all the silverware that had been at her place at the table on the floor. "Oops!" she said loudly, and bent to pick it up.

Lars reiterated in a firm voice, "We're not discussing this in front of the children."

Emma Beth was all eyes, but held her tongue.

The woman said in an abashed voice, "Oh. Oh, I see. All right. But if it was me, I couldn't go back there. I'd put that cabin on the market from over here, and go home."

Jill, straightening, put the silverware on her plate with a crash that threatened to break it. She said, still in that calm voice, "We aren't going to do that, and we aren't going to talk about it anymore."

Lars turned to Emma Beth and Airey. "Say, I don't know

about you, but I ate enough to need a walk to shake it down a little. Maybe I'll go down to the lake and see if there's a turtle to look at."

Despite her obvious interest in a conversation not meant for her ears, Emma Beth immediately slid off her chair. "Can I come, please, Daddy?"

"Sure. Airey, want to go for a walk?"

"Walk!" shouted Airey, struggling to escape the old-fashioned high chair that pinned him to the table.

Jill shot him a grateful look as Lars came and lifted his son out. "Let's go, partner."

As they went out the door, Emma Beth was heard to say, "Can we go to the turtle race?"

Back at the table, Jill winced. "Oh, I wish Lars hadn't said that magic word! But I'm sure he was thinking Emma Beth had forgotten all about the turtle races."

"Why not go?" asked the older woman. "The turtle races are fun. Each child gets a turtle of her very own to race. That little girl would just love it."

"I'm sure she would. But we have a lot to do at the cabin. I want to finish taking up the carpet and take the measurements of the bathroom so I'll know how much paint and tile to order."

The man said, "You're brave to even consider going ahead with that place. I'm sure it's bad luck out there."

"What happened was over a very long time ago and hasn't got anything to do with us."

The woman said, "I agree with Henry. Plus, I'd be afraid of ghosts."

Betsy said pragmatically, "There wasn't a ghost before we

discovered the bones, which is when you'd expect one. You know, trying to get his bones found—isn't that one reason ghosts walk? But now they are found and have been taken away, so there's no reason for him to come complaining."

Jill was amused. "Good thinking. Come on, Betsy, let's take a look at the morning."

The storm had cleared off overnight, leaving the air even more invigorating than before, if that were possible. Jill and Betsy went out and found it also very chilly. Jill reveled in the coolness, but Betsy, in a short-sleeved blouse and clam diggers, had apparently never gotten over living in California. She asked for a retreat to the downstairs lounge, where La-Z-Boy chairs waited.

"I can't wait till the propane heater is installed in our place," sighed Jill, selecting the leather chair. "That wood-burning stove is awful, almost as bad as washing in a single bucket of water in the morning."

"Jill, I didn't think you minded roughing it," teased Betsy, seating herself in the brocade-upholstered chair and pushing it back so it lifted her feet.

"I don't. If I'm going camping, all I want is a campfire and a tent; but if I'm staying in a house, I want a real stove and hot showers and electric lights."

Betsy laughed. "Me, too, except you can skip the part about camping." Then she sobered and said, "All right, the sound you just heard was the car of Henry and his nosy wife heading out. What did the investigators say about the skeleton? They didn't tell me anything."

"It's a human adult, possibly been there since 1944."

"Wow, they can tell that just by looking?"

"No, by the canning jars. Whoever canned those green beans wrote the date on strips of white adhesive tape and stuck them on the jars. All the jars down there are dated from 1944. There are no jars earlier or later than that."

"I see. So what you're deducing is that whoever was canning things ate 1943's veggies and didn't put any down there in 1945. Oh, Jill, could the skeleton be the canner herself? Maybe she fell down those steps and died there and no one knew it."

"Possibly, though at least one of the investigators thinks the skeleton is male. And the skull is broken in a couple of places, which shouldn't happen in a short fall onto a dirt floor."

"Murder?"

"Again, possibly." Disturbing thought, to have a murder victim in your vacation cabin. She said, "Want some coffee?" Wilma kept a coffeemaker in the lounge, and it was used by customers all day long. Jill rose and went to it, opening the cabinet door above it to find a mug.

"No, it'll get me all wired up," Betsy admitted.

Jill felt a stab of pity for her friend. She and Lars could refresh their energy levels with coffee any time of the day or night.

"What else did they find?" asked Betsy. "Besides the skeleton and jars of green beans, I mean."

"Buttons, mostly." Jill brought her mug of black coffee back to her recliner. "Different sizes, shirt and trouser buttons, all dark brown plastic. Investigator Mix showed them to Lars."

Betsy nodded. "I remember those little nubbins under the dust."

Jill continued, "Oh, and one odd thing. A kind of medallion shaped like an oval—" She curved her left thumb and forefinger into the left side of the shape. "Made of metal and stamped with a name on the top and bottom halves of it, with some numbers, like a serial number." It had been found under the bones; Mix had shown it to her.

"What was the name on it?"

"Dieter Keitel."

"Dieter? That's a very German name. And Keitel is, too, right?"

"Yes." Jill nodded.

"Are there a lot of Germans up in this part of the state?"

"A few. Up here there are mostly Finns, Norwegians, and Frenchmen."

"Frenchmen? In the frozen north?"

Jill smiled. "Ever hear of Quebec?"

"Oh. Well, yes."

"Some of the ones here are the descendants of the Voyageurs, those Frenchmen who engaged in the fur trade with the Indians back before this was a European country."

"Well, of course! I remember them from history books and romantic movies—funny, you think of them as living back then and forget their descendants might still be around. A lot of them married Indian women, didn't they?" But McElroy wouldn't be a descendant, not with that name.

"Yes, they did." Jill took a deep drink of her coffee and settled her bottom more comfortably in the chair. "I agree with you, they seem to have lived in a time and place all their own, you don't think of their descendants living in our time and place."

"I wonder if the skeleton is Dieter Keitel's?"

Jill said, "I have a list of all the people who owned this cabin, and none of them was named Keitel."

"Who owned the house in 1944?" asked Betsy.

Jill dug into her purse and came up with a notebook. She'd been required to carry one while a police officer and found it a habit worth keeping. She searched its pages and read aloud. "A couple named Helga and Matthew Farmer—he was a major in the U.S. Army. He bought it in 1940."

"How long did they own it?"

"Marsha and Arnold Nowicki bought it in 1945. They owned it until 1965 and sold it to Harry 'Buster' Martin."

"Not a Norwegian, Finn, or Frenchman on that list."

"No, this is a summer retreat, not a homestead."

"Yes. But not entirely. A root cellar with home-canned veggies would mean a primary residence, don't you think? Because if they were canning, they'd have planted a garden. Though on second thought, spending a winter in that cabin doesn't seem an attractive idea."

"Log cabins can be surprisingly snug, compared to a wooden house that's equally uninsulated. But you're right, it would still get awfully cold in there at night in the winter when all you've got for heat is a woodstove that needs constant feeding. You either get up every few hours or pile on the quilts." She remembered the stack of quilts in the chest. Maybe Betsy was right. "I wonder if we can find out if the Farmers used it year round?" She looked at her notes. "Buster Martin sold it to John Tallman in 1987, and it was the Tallman bankruptcy estate that sold the property to your New York Motto, who sold it to us."

"Who were the original owners?" asked Betsy.

"Well, it was built in 1904 for Mr. George Ferguson, who owned it until 1927, when he sold it to Mr. and Mrs. Harlan Ferguson—probably a son and daughter-in-law—and they're the ones who sold it to Major Farmer in 1940. He added what was probably his brand-new wife to the title in 1941."

"Hmmmm, you're right, no Keitels on the list of owners."

Jill said thoughtfully, "You know, the tag may have nothing to do with the skeleton. It may be one of those exchange things kids get into—remember friendship bracelets? I know penny arcades used to have machines that could stamp your name on medallions. Maybe two 'best friends' made them and gave them to each other—you know, as children. Then a child going down to fetch a jar of green beans for supper dropped it."

"Whose child?"

"Could be any one of them; the property title doesn't list children and there's no date on the tag. It might've been down there since Harlan Ferguson was a boy."

Betsy nodded. "Yes, of course. Was there anything else down there?"

Jill said, "Just the buttons."

Betsy thought for a minute. "Funny it wasn't picked up by one of the owners, if it was in the middle of the floor. Did the sheriff take it away with him?"

"Yes." Jill nodded.

"About those buttons—they were all alike?"

"Yes, but different sizes."

"Like from a uniform?"

Jill considered this. "No, Army buttons are made of

brass." Except on the shirts, of course. But none of these buttons were brass.

"How sure are they that the man—we're assuming he was a man—was murdered?"

"They wouldn't speculate for me, but they were treating it as a crime scene. They'll do a more thorough examination once they get the bones into a lab setting."

"Do they have a good lab up here?"

"The sheriff's department sends questionable bodies to Saint Paul for examination. They have the best facilities in the state." Her eyes half closed in thought. She wondered how they would send them down. If it were a body, they'd send it by funeral home wagon, but these were just loose bones. She said aloud, "They thought all the bones were there, and they took lots of photographs. It was interesting to see them at work; they took pictures before touching anything, of course, then they brushed the dust away and took more pictures, then recorded themselves picking up the pieces—for that, they brought in a video camera."

"Assuming the murderer was an adult, he must be at least in his eighties by now—if he's still around at all," said Betsy. "Or she."

"She?"

"Well, yes." Betsy continued, "Helga's husband was a major in the Army, right? So he could have been overseas, and she was here alone. If a prowler came by, broke in, it's possible she killed him in a fight."

Jill said, "Maybe she knew him. Maybe he was a neighbor." It was surprising how often that was true.

"How awful to think that! I suppose he came by thinking

to find a lonely woman looking for adventure. She had to disabuse him of the notion, and he got angry, and during the fight she whacked him on the head with a . . . a frying pan. You know, one of those big cast-iron ones. I've always thought one of those things would make a terrific weapon."

Betsy and her imagination! Still, "That would explain the skull injuries," said Jill, nodding.

Betsy smiled. "Of course, it could've been a baseball bat or a hammer—but a frying pan is more interesting, if you know what I mean. We're just letting our imaginations run free, right? I can see it happening at dinnertime, when she was in the kitchen cooking a meal."

"So why didn't she call the cops on him after she laid him out?"

Betsy sobered. "Because back in those days rape was a shameful thing, and in court they put the woman on trial as much as the man. Maybe she had seen him in town or while out on a walk and flirted with him."

"If what you're thinking is what happened, it would be more likely he was a stranger, don't you think? You couldn't just put a neighbor down in the cellar. He'd be missed."

Betsy said, "Yes, you're right, of course. It was a passing tramp, say, dirty and smelly. She put the body down the cellar, and the next day she ordered a roll of linoleum and sealed the floor. When her husband came home, she told him, and he ordered a second roll of linoleum and nailed it down along the wall with—what did Lars call that piece of wood around the base of the walls? Quarter round. Then they sold the place. Moved far away and left no forwarding address."

"That makes sense, I guess."

"Sure. That's why the linoleum was fastened down, to discourage the new owners from pulling it up."

"It's possible Helga never told Matthew, you know, if it was such a shameful thing. Maybe she wrote him a letter saying she just couldn't bear living out in the woods alone and was selling the place."

"Yes. In fact, that sounds more likely. Maybe she knew about quarter round edging on a floor. Or she hired someone to lay it professionally."

"Just to show that we're not speculating too wildly," noted Jill dryly, "how could we prove any of this?"

"I don't think anything can be proved. That's why we're letting our imaginations run free. It's what you do when you don't have any facts. When you have nothing but a skeleton in the cellar, and two layers of linoleum when the first one didn't look worn at all."

Jill looked thoughtful. "You're right about the linoleum. Though I thought the bottom pattern was ugly and it's possible she did, too, after she saw it laid. I painted our bedroom dark blue right after I married Lars, then went out the next day and bought another, lighter, less depressing color. So it's possible she got buyer's remorse and bought another pattern and didn't feel like tearing out the old one before laying the new one."

Betsy nodded. The lower layer of linoleum was a too-busy "moderne" pattern of muddy brown and dull green squares, ovals, and circles, while the upper one was a cheerful pattern of pink pebbles and gray stones. Of course, that first pattern might have been fashionable back then. Or were they wrong about when the linoleum was installed?

"Anyway, it's not just bones," said Jill. "There were the buttons. Buttons and bones."

"And a badge and a few jars of beans. Could the buttons be significant?"

Jill shrugged. "Lars said they looked like buttons in a jar his grandmother had.

Betsy asked, "Did you ever do any canning?"

"No, but I had an aunt who did. It seemed like an awful lot of work when canned or frozen peas were so cheap. She did it because her mother and grandmother had done it, and they taught her how. She baked her own bread, too."

"Now baking bread is different. Not so much work—and it's very satisfying to do. I don't really have time for it anymore, but I used to love to do it." Betsy sighed.

Jill remembered how her aunt's house smelled on the days she baked bread. "You'll have to show me how sometime. Then I'll bake for the both of us."

"What a splendid idea!"

They sat in comfortable silence for a little while. Then Betsy said, "I wonder who made those quilts you found in that trunk."

"Didn't I tell you? It was Mrs. Farmer. Helga. Her initials and the date are embroidered down in the corner of each one—except the last, which isn't a quilt but a crocheted rug."

"She crocheted a *whole rug*?"

"Yes, about four by three feet, a set of deep-pile squares connected by double crochet. Very attractive. It's at the bottom of the trunk. When we get back to the cabin, I'll show you."

The door to the upstairs opened and Wilma, owner of the camp, came in.

"I just got a phone call from the sheriff's department. He says you all can go back to your cabin now."

Betsy went out with Jill to find Lars down at the little beach showing the children how to skip stones across the water's surface. Emma Beth could throw pretty well, though skipping was beyond her. Airey could pick up a fistful of pebbles and sand and fling wildly. It would as often go sideways or even over his shoulder as into the water. He was dancing with excitement and shrieking with laughter after every fling.

"Airey scared the turtles away!" complained Emma Beth when she saw her mother approaching.

"I'm sorry to hear that," said Jill, though not with a great deal of sympathy. "Dear," she said to Lars, "we can go back to the cabin now."

They paid their bill, thanked Mrs. Griffin, and took the twenty-minute drive back to Thunder Lake.

Seven

BACK at the cabin, Lars got the ladder out of the shed and used it to climb up on the roof. Betsy winced at the sound his huge feet made on the wooden shakes—wasn't he damaging them?

Inside, Jill gave Emma Beth and Airey a set of bright-colored wooden blocks to play with on the back porch. Betsy watched the children quarrel cheerfully, then joined Jill in the kitchen as she built a fire in the stove. She said, "I went to one of those historical farms not long ago, where they do everything as it was done back in the 1800s, and the woman in the kitchen said she uses corn cobs to start her fires. Less work than chopping kindling."

"I'd remember that if I was going to keep this stove," said Jill. "There, that should be up to cooking temperature in half an hour or so. Ah, the good old days!"

Betsy laughed. "Come on, show me that crocheted rug."

Back out on the porch, Jill lifted the trunk's heavy lid and said, "Here, take a look at this. We were interrupted before we finished looking at the quilts."

She pulled out the Wedding Ring and Log Cabin quilts, laying them on the turned-back lid. Under them was a quilt covered with clusters of tiny hexagons made of pastel shades of pink, yellow, green, and blue fabric. "This pattern is called Grandmother's Flower Garden."

Betsy lifted a corner for a closer look. "Gosh, this is all hand stitched!" She unfolded it to see it was full size. "I wonder how many hours were invested in making this?"

"Hundreds, probably," replied Jill. "You used to see quilts like this at yard sales for five dollars, but nowadays people are waking up to the value of them." She pulled another quilt out of the chest, also full-size, whose squares were made up of four highly stylized birds with pointed wings and tails, each diving with its beak toward the center. "This is the bear paw pattern," said Jill, and Betsy adjusted her imagination accordingly. "It's also hand stitched—they're all hand stitched."

"Another reason to think someone lived here year round," noted Betsy. "What better way to occupy the winter hours than by making quilts?"

"Now, here's the rug," said Jill, lifting out an attractive article in cream-colored wool yarn about four feet long by three wide. The squares were made of dense loops, each loop a couple of inches long, each square about nine inches wide. The rug was soft to the touch.

"Ooooh," said Betsy, "I can just see this beside my bed, how sweet to step onto it with bare feet!" She ran the length of it through her fingers. "No tag or anything on it, so I guess it's handmade, too."

"And seeing it was in the chest with the quilts, it's hard not to think it was also made by Helga Farmer."

"You're sure it's crochet?"

"Yes, I recognize the flat areas between the looped squares. That's double crochet."

"So it is. How did she do those loops?" wondered Betsy, looking closer.

From outside came a piercing whistle: three rising notes.

"That's Lars calling us," said Jill. She turned and hurried to the front door, with Betsy at her heels. The children tumbled down the tower they were building and trotted after them.

Standing near the far side of the clearing was a woman, a little heavyset, dressed in a brown suede jacket, brown denim pants, and brown boots. Even her hair was a streaky brown that matched her outfit. She raised a tentative hand to them.

"It's the bear lady!" shouted Emma Beth.

"Hello there!" called Lars from up on the roof.

"Hello," the woman called back, but not loudly.

"Come on over!" called Jill, gesturing, and the woman obeyed.

"We're the Larsons," said Jill when the woman was close enough that shouting wasn't necessary. "Jill and Lars—he's the one on the roof—and Erik and Emma Beth. And this is our friend Betsy Devonshire."

"How do you do?" said the woman in a soft voice. "I'm Molly Fabrae, and my father used to own this cabin. We've been coming up to this area for years but I've never come over before. Never wanted to, really." Up close, the woman appeared to be in her later sixties, though she moved with the grace of a much younger woman.

"Was your maiden name Nowicki?" asked Jill.

"No, Farmer."

"Oh, we were just looking at some quilts your mother made!"

"You mean Helga, of course. She was my stepmother, *not* my mother." Her tone of voice made it suddenly clear why she had never visited the cabin.

"My father divorced my mother when I was four," she continued, "and I never saw my father again. He wrote a letter to me on my birthday every year until I was eight, then he disappeared. That was in 1944. It was quite a mystery, perhaps you've heard about it. The Army looked for him but couldn't find him."

"Did he go missing in action?" asked Betsy sympathetically.

"No. He was supposed to go overseas but he never got to his place of embarkation. No one knows what happened to him. My stepmother sold this place soon after he disappeared and she disappeared, too. Some people think he was a deserter, and she joined him wherever he was hiding and . . . well, that's a story they tell. I don't think it's true, though." She was looking around the clearing and then at the cabin, trying to sneak a peek at the inside through the screen door.

"Would you like to see inside?" asked Jill.

She hesitated, then said, "No, never mind, but thank you. I just wondered . . . You see, my father was a career soldier, a major who had done a lot of good things. He had joined the Army as a private and was promoted to corporal and then sergeant and then was sent to Officer Training School. He wouldn't be afraid to do his duty. So when I heard that a skeleton was found under the cabin, I was curious."

"Oh," Jill said, "I see. You think maybe . . ."

"Yes," said Molly, nodding. "I'm sure they have ways of identifying bones. I'm wondering if they'll tell you who the bones belong to, and if you would, in turn, tell me."

Lars, having come down the ladder, joined the conversation. "Why didn't you contact the sheriff's department on your own? I'm sure they would be very happy to talk to you about a possible identification."

"Oh, it's the sheriff's department I should contact. I didn't know who to call. I guess I was thinking there should be a police department in the area, but the address out here is Remer, and they don't have a police department."

"That's right," said Lars. "So it's the sheriff's department who is responsible for investigating. I can give you a name and a phone number, if you like."

"Yes, please. Thank you."

"You bet. I'll be right back." Lars went inside to search for a pen and slip of paper.

"You said you vacation up here," said Jill. "Where is your home?"

"We live in Saint Paul."

" 'We'?"

"My husband and I." She pulled a wry face. "We used to own a cabin on Long Lake but sold it to help put the kids through college, and somehow never bought another. But we miss coming up here, so a few years ago we began renting a cabin at

Anderson's Resort. I was walking close to your property, reminiscing about our old place. But I saw the two little children and realized I was trespassing and somehow lost my nerve."

"We thought you were a bear!" declared Emma Beth. "'Cause you're all brown!"

"Yes, I suppose I must have looked something like a bear," said Molly, smiling down at the child.

Jill said, "I hope the local law enforcement manages to put to rest what must be an unhappy memory for you."

"Yes, me, too."

Lars came back out with a business card. "This is all I could find to write on. That's my name and contact numbers on the front. The deputy investigator's name and number are on the back."

Molly took the card. "Thank you." Then she read the front of the card and glanced up at him in surprise.

He grinned at her. "Excelsior Police," he said, "but up here I'm just another civilian."

She smiled back, thanked them again, and departed.

"Poor lady," said Jill.

"You know, that's an explanation we never thought of," said Betsy. "That Helga batted her husband on his head."

"Mama, why would a lady hit her husband on his head?"

"Maybe because he was being naughty and asking too many questions. Like a silly little Em-Beth girl I know." Jill made a growly face and began to chase Emma Beth, who ran laughing back into the cabin.

* * *

THE lingering summer twilight had at last faded into darkness. The tourists had retreated to the resort or their cabins; the only sounds were of crickets and frogs and the occasional night bird.

Jill, Lars, and Betsy were sitting on the back porch, with Airey asleep on Jill's lap and Emma Beth determinedly awake on Lars's. The three adults were talking quietly.

"Turns cool when the sun goes down," noted Lars approvingly. "Better than air-conditioning."

"Good sleeping in air like this," agreed Betsy. "I can see why people buy cabins." She was thinking of Connor. How sweet it would be to have him sitting on a back porch like this, waiting for loons to sing! She tried to suppress a lonesome sigh.

"Cold in the winter, though," said Lars.

"In the winter we stay in town," said Jill.

"But what if they have some ski trails around here?" said Lars.

"Well, that might be different," said Jill. "We'll have to look into that. I hear these log cabins are fairly easy to keep above freezing if you install double-pane windows." Jill was an avid cross-country skier, and "above freezing" was her definition of comfortable.

"I can ski," said Emma Beth.

"So you can, darling, so you can."

A little silence fell. "Look, Mama, fireworks!" exclaimed Emma Beth.

A bright falling star was coming down the sky. It broke into three pieces, which quickly faded and were gone.

"Wow! That was amazing!" said Betsy.

"I've never seen a falling star do that," said Lars.

"It was beautiful," said Jill.

"Do it again," prompted Emma Beth.

"I'm afraid that's not something anyone can do on demand," said Jill.

Another silence fell, gradually moving from anticipatory—would there be another falling star?—to relaxed as the night settled in again.

It was suddenly broken by what seemed the brief, nervous titter of an old-fashioned comedy-act spinster. It was loud, and it echoed off the trees.

Betsy sat up straight. Was it what she thought?

Emma Beth said loudly, "Go 'way!"

"Hush, darling," said Jill.

The titter was repeated, and echoed by another spinster, then a third.

The loons.

The giggling went on for about half a minute then came the cry known as the "yodel." A rising note, broken into a higher register, then falling, a sound with all the sorrow of the world in it. It was repeated, and this time broke again at the high end into a third register.

Emma Beth began to cry. "Don't be afraid, honey," soothed Lars.

"I'm not afraid! But the loon is crying. Why is she crying, Daddy?"

"I don't know. Why do you think she's crying?"

"She's sad. She's crying 'cause she's sad."

"Does that make you sad, too?"

"Uh-huh."

"Me, too, just a little bit. But it's not a bad kind of sad. It's the kind of sad you feel when it's time for bed and you've had a busy day and you're all tired."

After a few seconds, Emma Beth sighed. "Yes," she said. "Go to bed, Looney!" she called out, her voice full of sympathy.

But the adults laughed anyway.

Eight

❖ ❖ ❖

THE next morning they discovered they had forgotten to pack the eggs. Jill had the stove all heated up, the coffee made, and the bacon frying—the air in the cabin smelled fantastically delicious—but there were no eggs to accompany it.

"I'll run over to The Wolf," announced Lars, meaning the general store about ten minutes away.

"May I come with you?" asked Betsy, afraid if she stayed she'd start sneaking the bacon—there was something about the northwoods air that did amazing things to the appetite. Not that hers needed encouraging.

"Sure," said Lars, and the two ran out to the SUV. It was a bright, sunny morning, and the air was still, if a little chilly. Betsy was glad she'd brought along her heavy flannel shirt.

The Lone Wolf was a shaggy clapboard building with at least two obvious additions to its original structure. Two old-fashioned gas pumps were out front, one with a faded cardboard OUT-OF-ORDER sign hanging from it.

Inside, on the left, was a huge old bar, but instead of liquor bottles it had coffee mugs and patent medicines on the mirrored shelves behind it. Six old men were gathered at the near end of the bar, drinking coffee and talking. "They had to restock that lake after them boys used dynamite all one summer to catch fish," one was saying. They fell silent as Lars and Betsy entered, then one said, "Larson, isn't it?"

"Yessir," said Lars. "We bought the old Buster Martin cabin. This is our guest for the weekend, Betsy Devonshire." He added to Betsy, "Wait here, I'll get the eggs," and hurried off to the right, where a row of chill boxes stood.

"Ms. Devonshire," said one old man, bald and plump, in a high, rough voice. "How do you like it up here in the northwoods?"

"Very much. It was thrilling to hear the loons last night."

"Say," said another man, small and very elderly, though his eyes were keen. He lifted a gnarled hand and said, "Wasn't it the Farmer cabin where they found that skeleton yesterday?"

"Yes," said Betsy.

"Thought so. I bet I know who it was."

The other men turned on their stools to look at him. "You mean you been sitting there for the past half hour and never said a word about that?" demanded the plump man indignantly.

"Been waitin' to get a word in edgewise," retorted the little man. He went on in an old-fashioned Minnesota accent, pulling out some vowels and changing *th*s into *d*s. "Maybe some o' yoo-oo remember dere was a German POW who

escaped from a camp near here an' dey never found 'im?" Two
of the old men nodded, and the little man continued, "They
had five men walk away from there, you betcha, an' caught
four of 'em. Two built a raft, they was going to float down
the Mississippi to New Orleans an' stow away on a ship back
to Europe. Saw a big city an' t'ought they was there, heh,
heh, heh." His laugh was soft and high-pitched. "But they
was in Minneapolis. I guess they didn't realize what a big
country this is. The other two was found in the woods a
couple miles from the camp," he continued. "But one was
never found at all. I was fourteen, maybe fifteen years old at
the time and I remember he had a funny first name. It
was . . ." He thought deeply, the crinkles on his forehead and
around his eyes deepening into folds. "Jeeter? No. I remember it rhymed with Peter, but it wasn't Peter."

"Well, isn't that interesting," said Lars, who could move
silent as a ghost, and was suddenly behind Betsy.

The little man started and gestured sharply. "You betcha.
They published his picture in the paper and put up posters,
but they never found 'im. My Aunt Pauline told me a bear
probably got 'im, it was in the late summer he ran off, and
that time of year them bears are eating anything they can get
a paw around to put on weight for their hibernation."

"My grandmother told me a bear ate a dishtowel she had
drying on the line one autumn," offered the largest old man.
He had small, sad eyes, a long nose, and scanty white hair.

The little man said, "That ain't the point; the point is, I
bet that skeleton is the missing German soldier."

"Awww!" scoffed the fat man.

But the others were silent, thinking this over.

Betsy was amazed by this conversation. "What were German soldiers doing in Minnesota?" she asked.

"Well, they had to put 'em somewhere!" replied the little man. "We was turning the tide in North Africa, capturing thousands of 'em. But Europe was still overrun by Germany, except for England, an' England couldn't take 'em all—and besides it was looking like Germany was going to invade. So they packed 'em onto ships an' brought 'em over here. Just about every state had camps set up for them, I heard. I read somewhere that most of 'em were converted Civilian Conservation Corps camps."

The largest old man said, "I remember my dad went to CCC over at Remer in the thirties. He used to talk about cutting trail and building shelters in this very state park."

The littlest old man thrust in, "You bet, and during World War Two they repaired them camps and built fences around them and brought captured Germans to them. Italians and Japs, too, though I never heard of any of them in Minnesota."

"But wasn't that dangerous, bringing combat soldiers to America?" asked Betsy.

The little man snorted. "Not really. They took away their weapons, o' course, and made 'em wear clothes with big letters *PW* painted on 'em, set guards on 'em—not that they needed guarding. Brought to the middle of this great big country—where was they goin' to run to?"

Betsy thanked the men for the information, and they went out to the SUV.

On the ride back, Betsy said, "So that badge they found in the cellar . . ."

Lars said, "I'm betting it's some kind of ID tag. It didn't look like a dog tag, but maybe they were issued them at the camp—or maybe their own dog tags didn't look like ours." He fell into a thoughtful silence. "You know," he said after a while, "it was a double badge, with the same name and some numbers on the top and bottom of it, and what looked like a row of dashes cut across its middle, maybe so you could break it in half. That's not a bad way to do a dog tag; our way, making two of them, means they clattered every time you moved." Lars, unsurprisingly, was a former Marine.

Betsy, more surprisingly, was a former WAVE. She nodded, remembering how noisy they could be. Less so for the females, who could tuck them into a bra.

"Why two of them anyhow?" asked Jill a little while later, over bacon and eggs scrambled with sweet peppers and onions—plain for the children.

Betsy and Lars looked at each other. "In case you get, um, terminated," said Lars at last. "Someone, on his way somewhere else, finds you in the field and takes one dog tag as proof you're, um, and leaves the other one with you for easy identification."

"Oh," said Jill, now aware this was not a suitable topic with the little pitchers present. "More coffee?"

"None for me, thanks," said Emma Beth in a perfect imitation of an adult.

Betsy choked back a laugh. Emma Beth took herself seriously and perhaps it was cruel to show amusement when her dignity was on display.

"Do you think it's really possible Dieter Keitel was here at the cabin back in the forties?" Jill asked, carefully avoiding saying scary words like "die" and "skeleton."

"I guess so," said Lars. "The question is, what was he doing here?"

"Is Dieter a friend of ours?" asked Emma Beth.

"No, darling, he's someone who may have visited this cabin back before even your father was born."

Imagining a time that long ago was beyond Emma Beth's ability, so she returned her attention to her eggs. "'Kay," she murmured.

"Nice!" announced Airey, waving his spoon.

"What's nice?" asked Lars.

"Aaaaaae-guh!"

"Well, we're glad you approve. Now eat it all up."

" 'Kay," he said, very satisfied to find himself in a place where an echo of his big sister's reply was appropriate.

"Maybe nobody was home when he got here," suggested Betsy.

"Then who, um, terminated him? He didn't hurt himself falling down those stairs, not with wooden steps and a dirt floor at the bottom. There were three fractures, remember."

"Three?" said Betsy.

"Two on his head and one to his right arm."

"Wow. All right, he ran into someone here."

"I runned into Minnie at The Common," announced Emma Beth, paying attention again.

"Ran into Minnie. Yes, you did, silly girl, not watching where you were going."

"I fell down and hurt my knee."

Airey made a sound like a car engine being gunned, his version of scornful laughter, and waved his spoon. "Faw down!"

The adults surrendered and focused on the children and their own breakfasts.

They had barely finished clearing away the breakfast things when there was the sound of a vehicle coming into the clearing. Lars looked out the front window and said, "Uh-oh."

"Is the sheriff back again?" asked Jill, dismayed.

"No, the media."

"Oh, no!"

"Not going to talk to them?" asked Betsy, hurrying to the window to peer out.

"Not on your life," said Jill. "Up here we are private citizens and prefer to remain that way."

A big white van with a satellite dish on top of it and a television station logo on its side was in the clearing. Men and women had emerged, one with a television camera on his shoulder, another with a furry microphone on a boom, yet another in a close-fitting suit, her perfect hairdo being blown a trifle awry by a vagrant breeze.

After they got set up, the woman stepped in front of the little porch and Betsy could hear her say, "On me in three, two, one . . . This is your KCCT reporter Marla Johnson from the scene where a human skeleton was discovered in a root cellar yesterday. Sheriff Randy Fisher refuses to speculate on the identity of the skeleton or how it came to be under this cabin." Pause. "Cut."

The man with the camera let its nose drop toward the ground, and Ms. Johnson turned to knock on the door.

Lars opened it and came out, and the camera came up again. The reporter said, "Good morning. I'm Marla Johnson—"

Lars interrupted her in a voice that brooked no argument.

"We have nothing to say. Please clear off our property. Thank you." He turned and came back inside.

The reporter blinked at the closed door then turned to face the camera. "That was Lars Larson, new owner of the cabin in which—*under* which the skeleton was found."

She tried knocking on the door again, but it stayed shut. She looked around and saw Betsy at the window, but Betsy immediately withdrew.

The crew filmed the cabin from various angles and went away.

Lars, Betsy, and Jill spent the rest of the morning working to clear the beautiful white pine floor of its coverings of linoleum and musty carpet. The floor—whose wood looked more yellow than white to Betsy—appeared to be in good shape, no stains or severe scuffing. Twice cars appeared in the clearing bringing members of news agencies. Lars patiently repeated his initial reply to their request for an interview.

Between visits the cabin was emptied of the carpet and linoleum coverings. Then the bathroom walls and floor were diagramed and measured. After a light lunch—spent ignoring the persistent knocking of another television crew—Lars said, "The heck with this. Emma Beth, my little sweetheart, how would you like to go see the turtle races?"

The child's face flushed pink and her mouth opened with delight, her light blue eyes fairly shooting sparks. "Can we go? Can we go right now? We should go right now so they won't be over and we've missed them."

"Right now," said Lars.

Everyone piled into the SUV, and Lars, his foot a trifle heavy on the accelerator, took them out to Highway 6, down the other side of Thunder Lake, and past the shore of Big Rice Lake. He drove right by Laura Lake, between Upper Trelipe and Little Bass Lake, split Inguadona Lake, came within hailing distance of Rice Lake and Cooper Lake and on to the shore of Girl Lake—and Longville. All in less than twenty minutes and without even nearing all the lakes in the area.

Longville was a pleasant little town with very broad streets and lots of shops catering to tourists. Lars found the street with the statue of the turtle, correctly surmising that it marked the site of the races about to begin. There was already a crowd gathering and he had to park in a lot two long blocks away.

The "racetrack" was two circles painted in the middle of the broad street, one about four feet in diameter, the other circling it, about eight yards across. A low stage had been set up alongside it, fronted by five-gallon buckets filled with annoyed or frightened or confused turtles. On the stage, a man with a microphone was encouraging children to come forward and, for an entry fee of three dollars, select a turtle to race. All the turtles, he said, were fresh caught and would be released at the end of the day. "No professional racers allowed," he asserted, mock seriously.

Airey picked the first turtle he saw and promptly dropped it onto the asphalt when it came out of its shell and scratched his fingers lightly with its claws. Betsy picked it up and tried to interest him in it. He was willing to look, but not anxious to take it back. It was a lively, good-size turtle, so Betsy kept it for him.

Emma Beth, on the other hand, was looking for a soul mate and went peering into bucket after bucket. She was on the last one before a turtle looked back at her with what she interpreted as a friend-for-life eye.

The rules of the races were simple. For each heat, a child placed his or her turtle inside the smaller circle, holding it in place until the command to start was given. The first turtle to cross the border of the outer circle won.

The turtles, new to the game and in any case not particularly interested in racing toward a shouting crowd of humans, mostly retreated to the security of their shells and refused to move. Others went in fits and starts. One or two wandered at random inside the larger perimeter. But occasionally, and inevitably, one would manage to cross the yellow line, to the cheers of its temporary owner—and sometimes the tears of a loser.

Airey's turtle was the vague sort—it set off with a will, but quickly lost its compass and began to draw a meandering line that never approached the finish.

Emma Beth's turtle set off in a determined straight path that should have made it the winner. But there was another turtle that apparently had grasped the rudiments of the competition and set off in a fast scramble for the border, crossed it, and nearly vanished into the crowd before its delighted owner could retrieve it. Emma Beth's soul mate finished second.

Jill made everyone who had handled the turtles wash their hands before taking them to the ice-cream shop for a consolation ice-cream cone.

Nine

ICE-CREAM cones eaten, they all lingered to watch more races. The crowd cheered the turtles on, and a small group of rowdies got busy taking side bets.

"Excuse me," said a female voice, and Betsy looked around to see a slender woman about her own height, with hair dyed a chocolate brown with blond streaks in it. Her face was lined, but her broad smile revealed good teeth, and her blue eyes were shining. Jill took the childrens' free hands, prepared to retreat if the woman proved to be a reporter.

"I'm Johanna Albright. Are you the people who found that skeleton in your root cellar?"

"Why do you ask?" said Jill, taking two steps back while looking around for a photographer.

"Because if you are, then I imagine you are also looking for information about the German POW camps in this area, and I know almost everything about them."

Lars said, "Who told you we wanted to know about the German POW camps?"

The woman waved her hands impatiently. "It's all over town that the skeleton is probably that German prisoner who ran off from one of the camps back in 1944 and was never found."

"Where were the camps, do you know?" asked Betsy.

"There was one right in the area. I'm from here; I actually remember seeing German soldiers working in Longville. They painted our city hall. They were very handsome, I remember my mother and older sisters talking about how good-looking they were. They weren't treated badly, my mother said a neighbor used to bake treats for them, and they had soccer competitions and wood carving contests with other camps. I have a memory of them going by in the back of a great big truck one winter, going to the forest to cut down trees. They waved at us and we waved back. They were only here for about a year, two winters and a summer. Then the war was over and they were shipped back home. They were all afraid of the ruin their country was left in. Some of them got engaged to women here so they could stay in America."

Johanna was bubbling over with information, which she shared with smiling enthusiasm.

"Here," said Jill, noticing that people were beginning to eavesdrop, "let's get out of this crowd. Is there a place we can sit down?"

With the crowd thinning, there were two vacant tables outside in front of the ice-cream shop. Lars led the way to the farther one, taking two chairs from the nearer so everyone could sit. The table and chairs were metal, spray-painted aqua and cream. The chair legs squealed on the concrete patio as they were pulled out and everyone sat down.

"It's nice of you to volunteer to talk with us," said Jill. "I'm Jill Larson, this is my husband Lars, this is our friend Betsy Devonshire, and these are our children Emma Beth and Erik."

"I'm so glad I found you!" gushed Johanna. "I was afraid you'd get away before I had a chance to talk to you. I'm the local expert on the camps. I've written articles about them and everything."

"How did you find out about the skeleton?" asked Lars.

"Well, it was all over the news last night, so anyone who didn't already know found out then. But some of us knew before the news came on. It was Mavis Johnson who told me over lunch at the coffee shop about it probably being that lost German POW. I don't know where she heard it, but when I told Allie Burnside after lunch, she'd heard that, too."

Betsy smiled; the famous Excelsior grapevine was not the sole member of its species.

"Do you remember some of the German prisoners running away?"

"Oh, yes. Well, I remember the grown-ups talking about it. My father said two of them built a raft to float down the Mississippi on, intending to get to New Orleans and stow away on a ship bound for Europe. They drifted at night and slept in the fields by day and after many days came to this big city and were pleased they'd made it. But it was only to Saint Paul, where they were caught and sent back. They had no idea this was such a big country, you see." She chuckled, and shook her head at the ignorance of the two unlucky POWs.

"What about the one who was never captured?"

"Yes, isn't that interesting that they've found that skeleton in that cellar? Do you suppose they really are his bones?"

"I think we're going to have to wait for the police to finish investigating before we know for sure whose bones they are."

"Mama, can I have some more ice cream?" asked Emma Beth, exceedingly bored by this conversation.

"May I have some more ice cream, and no, you may not."

Betsy asked, "Do you know where the POW camp around here was located?"

"Down on a lakeshore, Woman Lake, I think. I understand there are ruins of the old barracks, nearly hidden among raspberry bushes. But you shouldn't go for a look because this time of year there are lots of bears in there eating the ripe berries."

"Do you know anything about the Army major who disappeared about the same time?" asked Jill.

Johanna frowned over that for a brief while. "I remember hearing about it years later, not at the time—I was just a little girl, and either the talk went sailing over my head, or they didn't talk about it in front of us children. It was apparently quite a scandal—but that happened in the winter. I remember them saying something about him catching a train in a snowstorm, and the POW who never got found ran away in the summer."

So much for Betsy's forming theory that the murder of Dieter Keitel and Major Farmer's disappearance were related. She sighed.

Johanna continued, "My mother told me the talk at the time was about how much older he was than his wife. I think he realized he'd made a big mistake marrying her. He wasn't from around here, you know. He came up to inspect the paper factory that was making cardboard for the Army. It was one of those love-at-first-sight things that sometimes happens to older men who meet pretty young blondes. She was a high school dropout, working as a waitress right here in Longville, but really good-looking. She played him for a fool, and when he realized what he'd done, he just walked out on her."

"I see," said Lars.

"Yes, it's a sad story," said Johanna, catching something in Lars's tone and changing her own gossipy tone to one of regret.

Jill asked, "What about Mrs. Farmer selling the cabin? Do you know when that happened?" That would be a test question, Betsy thought, because the date of the sale would be something Jill either knew or had access to. Good for Jill, thought Betsy.

But Johanna didn't know exactly when that happened. "She was the subject of a lot of talk, of course, poor kid. She stuck it out until the following spring or summer, I think. And even after she left, some said she went off to join him wherever he was hiding out. In any case, neither of them was ever heard from again."

Yet if there was no connection, thought Betsy on their way back to the car, why was the unfortunate Dieter Keitel found in the Farmers' root cellar?

Did Helga Farmer live with that body in the basement all those months until she could join her runaway husband? Is it possible she didn't know about it? Then why put down the linoleum to cover over that trapdoor? Is it possible beautiful white pine floors were not seen as beautiful in those days? Betsy recalled how fashionable it once was to cover hardwood floors with wall-to-wall carpeting, just as now it was to uncover them again.

And was it true Major Farmer ran away because he'd come to realize the hideous mistake he'd made marrying the beautiful Helga? Then why did she sell the cabin and move to join him in his hiding place?

She thought of Molly Fabrae, who was sure her father would not run away and who had hoped the skeleton in the root cellar would put to rest an old canard.

She sat back in the car seat to think. Suppose the German soldier came to the Farmer cabin, which was probably even more isolated then than it was now, and held Helga Farmer captive—until her husband came home? Then, say, there was a fight, which the POW lost?

No, because they'd surely report it. No need to hide the body and flee the scene.

She was out of speculations; she couldn't think what might have happened. To quote Godwin quoting Mark Twain, it was too many for her.

* * *

Bᴀᴄᴋ at the cabin, they closed everything up, packed their belongings, and set off for home.

There was no discussion of the case. The overtired kids were too distracting all the way down Highway 169, whining and complaining and crying. And of course, the law made it impossible for Jill to take Airey out of his carrier seat and hold him in her lap, so he had to be left to his own very slender collection of self-comfort methods.

Betsy held his hand, which helped only a little. Emma Beth wanted her hand held, too, between snits and complaints that the car was too hot or too cold or the trip was too long. They both fell asleep just as the exit for Highway 7 came up, less than ten minutes from home.

So Betsy was very tired on reaching her apartment that evening. Her message light was blinking but she decided she was not up to calling anyone back and instead made herself a light supper and went to bed.

"Hᴇ came in once, he called once," announced Godwin on his arrival at Crewel World the next morning.

"Who? Oh, Connor," said Betsy.

"Well, done!" said Godwin. "Atta girl. You really sounded like you actually had forgotten him."

"Of course I haven't forgotten him." She smiled. "I had forgotten we had a quarrel, though. Funny what an old skeleton can do to your priorities."

"About that skeleton—"

"Later. What happened in the shop while I was away?"

"That small order of wool floss from The Gentle Art is

nearly sold out with one repeat buyer already, so I placed a bigger order—it's on the desk," replied Godwin obediently. "The order of kits of napkins and table runners with stamped autumn leaves came in, and I called Marge to see how close she is to finishing the model for us. She should bring it in by the end of the week. Which reminds me, we need to brainstorm about what we want to put in our autumn window. The display needs to go up soon. The back-to-school sales are in full swing, and I was wondering if we couldn't tie into that theme somehow. You know, featuring our classes. Which further reminds me. Look at this." Godwin went back behind the desk, which served as a checkout counter in the shop, and came up with a bundle of white tissue paper held together by string tied in a bow.

He untied it to reveal a scarf knit in a yarn drifting in lovely shades of blue from aqua to pinky lavender. But what drew the eye was the stitch used. It looked like weaving using two strands. No, it looked like the backside of the basketweave stitch. Betsy turned it over. The underside of the knitting didn't look a whole lot like any pattern she'd ever seen. She turned it back to look at the interesting cross-hatching on the face.

"Who did this?" she asked.

"Peggy Dokka. She has an old book of knitting patterns and found this in it. She wants to teach a class. She says it's not a difficult stitch, you can learn it in one session."

"Let's tell her yes, and I'll be the first to sign up."

"Too late," said Godwin with a chuckle.

"I like the idea of a back-to-school window. How many

classes are we offering this fall?" asked Betsy. "There's that one on needlepoint, where we teach six stitches—we'll need only four people to make up the class, right? Rosemary is going to do her sweater class, Peggy can teach this scarf, and you can do an adult crochet class. We'll need at least one advanced class, maybe one on candlewicking?"

"Careful, or we won't have anything left to offer over the winter," counseled Godwin.

"I was thinking we could offer a class on the Three Kings this winter. It's a counted pattern, I can't remember what catalog I saw it in. Very elaborate robes on the kings, with beads and cords, worked on hand-dyed linen. I'll have to get out my catalogs and hunt for it. If we start it soon, most of the class will have it completed by Christmas."

"Yes, but they won't be able to get it finished before Christmas. Heidi wants Christmas projects in by Thanksgiving." Heidi specialized in washing, stretching, and framing fine needlework pieces, or turning them into pillows, a process called finishing.

Godwin continued, "And I saw that pattern, it's gorgeous. So it isn't something you'd try finishing yourself. All right, I'll find it, and we'll offer it maybe in the spring of next year."

Betsy asked, "Anything else?"

The phone began to ring.

"The Monday Bunch wants you to talk to them about the skeleton."

"All right, but I don't have a lot to say." Betsy picked up the cordless phone that stood on the library table in the middle of the front part of the shop. "Crewel World, Betsy speaking, how may I help you?"

"Betsy, it's Jill."

"Hi, Jill, have you recovered from the drive home?"

"Yes, thank you, and so have the children. I hear the sheriff's department of Cass County has announced that the bones belong to one Corporal Dieter Keitel, late of the Army of the Third Reich."

"Well, that's not a surprise, is it?"

"They did it without sending the bones to Saint Paul."

"Is that a bad thing?"

"Depends on what they found to convince them. One thing is that ID tag, it really is a World War Two German dog tag. But there's something else, they gave his age—he was just twenty."

"Oh, that's sad!"

"As for not sending the bones to Saint Paul, Lars thinks they might not bother, if they're really sure. It's probably a cash-saving thing. Cass County isn't exactly the richest county in the state, and budgets are being slashed all over. Anyway, who else's bones could they be?"

"Which doesn't answer the question: How did they come to be in your root cellar?"

"That's a question I'd like to ask Helga Farmer. I wonder what became of her?"

"Yes, the fact that she was never heard of again is suspicious, isn't it?" Betsy tapped a pencil on the table, thinking.

"She was never heard from up there. For all we know, she's fine, living in her retirement home in Arizona this very day."

"I wonder if the sheriff is going to try to find her."

"I wonder if you and I could find her."

"Are you serious?" Betsy stopped tapping.

"I don't like unexplained bones in my cellar. Besides, remember Molly Fabrae? She'd like to know what became of her father. I can't help but think Helga Farmer might be able to tell us."

Ten

❖ ❖ ❖

At one, after a very busy morning, Betsy sent Godwin to Sol's Deli next door for ham and Swiss sandwiches on rye, potato chips, and their famous crisp kosher dill pickles.

The deli was old, probably original to the building, which was built in the early twentieth century, with a white tile floor set here and there with black squares, a pair of tiny wire-legged tables with three chairs apiece, and old-fashioned slant-front glass cases in back where meats and cheeses were on display, ornamented with pickles and olives of every kind and color.

Standing in front of one of the cases was Connor. Under his direction, the owner, a bald, tired-looking man with a potbelly sagging into his apron, whose name was not Sol, was building a submarine sandwich.

Godwin came up behind Connor, calling his name. "Oh, I'm so glad you are here! I've been wanting to talk with you."

"What about?" Connor smiled back at him.

"Betsy." Both men's smiles vanished at the same time.

"Serious?" asked Connor.

"Very."

"All right. Just a minute." He took the wrapped sandwich in its white paper bag, paid for it, and went to one of the little tables.

Godwin gave his order and said he'd wait right over there for it, and joined Connor at the table.

"What's this about?" asked Connor as Godwin sat down.

"I told you: Betsy. What are your intentions?"

"What are you, her father?"

"Something more important: her friend."

"All right, fair enough. My intentions are honorable. Okay?"

"She's very unhappy right now, over you."

"I'm unhappy as well. A certain amount of rough passage is to be expected when two very independent people past a certain age and burdened with their separate histories try to mesh. We'll work it out."

"When?"

"When the time is right. I hope you aren't the interfering kind, Goddy."

"Of course I am! How *could* you expect otherwise?"

Connor tried to hide a smile. "That's a valid point. So what are you proposing?"

"I think you should talk to her."

"I don't think she's ready to talk to me."

"You don't know her. She'll let you get away rather than be the first to speak. Come on, let's go back."

"What about my lunch?"

"Bring it along."

Bᴇᴛsʏ looked up when Godwin came back, and saw there was a man right behind him.

Connor.

Betsy couldn't think of what to say and so said nothing.

Apparently Connor was in the same state; he simply stood by the long white counter that held knitting materials, looking at her. His eyes were kind, but he said nothing.

Godwin strode to the library table and put down the big white paper bag. "Isn't anyone going to say hello?" he asked.

"Hello, Betsy," said Connor in his pleasant baritone.

"Hello, Connor," said Betsy, feeling her face getting warm. But silence fell again.

Godwin sighed. "All right, say you're sorry." He looked at both of them.

"I'm sorry," said Betsy.

Connor took a step forward. "I'm sorrier than you, for you were right. My shameless daughter has admitted she would prefer I not see you anymore."

"What are you going to do about that?" asked Godwin.

"I've told her that she is forever my favorite child but that I'm an adult man, happily divorced from her mother, and seeing another woman I like very much."

"What did she say?" asked Betsy.

"That she'll start a novena to the Blessed Virgin to bring me to my senses and meanwhile not say another word to me about you."

Godwin laughed but Betsy said, "Doesn't it make you uncomfortable to know someone's nagging heaven on your behalf? It would me."

"Oh, she's always nagging heaven on my behalf, convinced every ship I went to sea on was going to sink, every cargo I carried would turn out to be contraband, every crew I led would mutiny. She thinks if it weren't for her novenas, I'd be drowned or arrested or in prison. May I join you for lunch? I brought my own sandwich." He held up a white paper bag.

"Of course," Betsy said.

The three sat down at the table.

As had become a usual practice, Betsy swapped half her potato chips for Godwin's big dill pickle. Bites were taken and "yums" were murmured.

Then Godwin said, "All right, now we're all friends again, and it was all my doing, I feel I deserve a reward. Tell me about the skeleton."

"What skeleton?" Connor asked.

"What did the newspaper say?" Betsy asked.

"That the skeleton of a man was found under a log cabin newly purchased by Jill and Lars Larson."

"Uh-oh," said Connor, who could go for days without opening a newspaper or catching a local television news program.

Godwin continued, "That it appeared to be an old skeleton, not something left there last winter. That's about it. So who found it? Do you know who it is? Was it murder or an accident? Jill said something when she called here, didn't she?"

"Yes, the sheriff's department announced that it's the

mortal remains of Dieter Keitel, a German POW. Jill found his bones when she uncovered a trapdoor in the floor." Betsy described the event.

"Dear God," said Connor. "The things you get into."

"So you saw the skeleton, too?" asked Godwin.

"Yes. It was covered in a thick coat of dust, hardly scary at all."

"But was it an accident or murder?"

"There are some broken bones, especially on the skull, that shouldn't have happened in a fall down that short flight of stairs onto a dirt floor. So probably murder. Dieter walked away from the POW camp in the late summer of 1944. Connor, he was only twenty years old."

"Just a kid," said Connor, looking thoughtful.

Godwin frowned a little, thinking. "You know, if he hadn't died back then, he'd be eighty-seven today."

Betsy said, "What does that mean?"

"I don't know. But something, somehow." Godwin ate a potato chip. "Makes me wonder if it's better to die young and leave a beautiful corpse or to live and wind up a wrinkled old man."

"You'd better hurry and make up your mind," said Betsy, and Connor laughed.

When they had finished their meal, Connor said to Betsy, "I'm glad we're friends again. May I see you this evening?"

"Well, I've got a class tonight, then some bookkeeping to do . . ."

"All right, I understand," said Connor. He did not ask about the next night, but said good-bye and left.

"And you were looking so good to him," said Godwin.

"What?" she said, exasperated. "I do have a class tonight."

"You should have suggested he come over for a nightcap. No wonder the good ones always get away from you—you have no idea how to manage a love affair."

J ILL came in near closing time with the two children, all restored to sunny-bright moods. "Lars called the sheriff's department investigator up in Walker to see what made them decide the skeleton was Dieter Keitel, and guess what?"

"What?" replied Betsy.

"They found the records kept by the old sheriff back in the 1940s, and he actually had put away an official description from the POW camp medical officer, and a copy of the wanted poster, with a photograph on it. He kept them because, we suppose, the case was never solved. Did you notice the gold tooth in the skull?"

"Yes." Betsy nodded.

"Well, it's mentioned in the poster. Something like, 'a gold crown on a molar on the right side near the front, noticeable when he talks or smiles.'"

Betsy sat down abruptly. "Oh, my."

"What's the matter?"

"I don't know. 'Noticeable when he talks or smiles'—that makes him a real person, not an anonymous skeleton. Now I feel as if I've seen him naked and I'm embarrassed. He was just a kid, Jill, all of twenty, dragged off first to war, then to the middle of another country, surrounded by people he was taught to think of as the enemy."

"Yeah, people who waved at him as he was hauled around

in a big truck, and who brought him treats and taught him crafts, and let him organize soccer tournaments."

The fist that had been squeezing Betsy's compassionate heart loosened. "Yes, of course you're right. C. S. Lewis said that about the English during the war: they'd declare hanging was too good for their enemies, then give tea and biscuits to the first injured German pilot who turned up in their back garden."

Godwin said, "But someone didn't give this guy a cup of tea and a cookie. Instead he got a knock on the head."

"That's right," said Jill. "And I want to ask you, Betsy, to use your sleuthing talent to help me find out what happened."

"Now, wait a minute. First of all, there's an official police investigation going on right now. They know the land, they know the people, and they have the proper tools. And second, it's three hours to Longville. I've got a business to run right here in town. I can't go running up to Cass County to look into this every time I get a clue."

"Mama, Mama?" asked Emma Beth. "Are you going to buy floss?"

"Not today, sweetie."

"Can I go look at the floss?"

"Floss!" agreed Airey.

"Here, I have a better idea," said Betsy, who did not want a pair of unsupervised children pulling expensive and carefully sorted silk floss from spinner racks as if they were undecorating a Christmas tree. She went into the deepest drawer in her checkout desk and came up with two pieces of bubble wrap. "Who wants to help me pop some bubbles?" she asked.

"Me, me!" shouted the children.

"You have to sit by yourselves at the table while you're doing this job for me, okay? Honestly, I don't know where all this stuff keeps coming from. I'm so glad I have you two to help me out."

In about half a minute the two were seated at the library table in the middle of the room, making snapping noises, totally engrossed.

"It's not just Cass County we want to look at," said Jill to Betsy. "We need to find out what happened to Mrs. Farmer—and probably her husband, too. They could be anywhere."

"And this will make it easier?"

"No, it means we use our computers."

"'We'? 'Our' computers?"

"I want us to work together. You can tell me where to look, and what to look for, and I can save you time by doing the work. Together we can figure this thing out."

"I don't know . . ."

"Well, I'm going to try it on my own, regardless. But I'm sure I'll do better with your help."

Betsy smiled. "I believe you'll be disappointed if the Cass County Sheriff's Department gets there first."

Jill shook her head. "No, I won't. I don't care who gets there first, so long as someone gets there. If they figure it out, that's great with me. But I don't want them to find it hard to solve and gradually let it slide, until we find ourselves with a cold trail."

Betsy laughed. "Jill, this trail is already about as cold as it can be. Not so far from seventy years cold, in fact. All the adults who might have known something useful are dead."

"Not all of them. Johanna, for one. I doubt she's the only one."

Betsy remembered the old men gathered at the bar in The Lone Wolf General Store, and nodded. "All right, not all of them. But it'll be hard to find the time to go all the way back up there to talk with them."

"I have a feeling I'm going to be working some extra hours pretty soon," said Godwin, but not too unhappily. He loved being on the inside of Betsy's cases, the first to know of clues discovered and conclusions formed. And Betsy, for her part, was careful to keep that bargain in mind.

"I can do the legwork, too, or most of it," said Jill. "But where do we start?"

"With Helga, I suppose," said Betsy after a moment's thought. "Where did she go? Why did she go? Is she still alive?" She thought some more. "If I had to throw away everything I had here and run off . . . well, that would be hard. I could sell the business—to Godwin probably."

"Hurrah!" said Godwin. "Not that I want you to do any such thing, but hurrah for thinking of me."

Betsy ignored him and said to Jill, "So maybe Helga sold the cabin to a friend."

"Arnold and Marsha Nowicki," said Jill. "They're the next owners listed."

"Do we know where they're from? Or where they are now?"

"No, but we can find out, I suspect via the Internet."

"What do you think the Nowickis can tell us? If they weren't friends with the Farmers."

"You know how people talk while they're waiting to sign

papers," said Jill, remembering. " 'So, where are you going from here?' the buyer may ask. 'Oh, we bought a farm in Wisconsin, not far from the Dells.' Like that."

"Not bad," Betsy said. "You may be right. And say, another place to look would be family. I wonder if Helga had any siblings. My sister and I weren't terribly close, but when I needed a place to stay after I divorced Hal the Pig, I knew how to contact her. I would think Helga would know how to contact her sibling or siblings. We can do the same, but we'll need to find out Helga's maiden name. One way to do that would be to research her husband's military record—I know that's available on the Internet. I have a customer who is a genealogy nut and she did that to find out about her great-grandfather's military service. If we can find out where he was stationed when they married, then I'll bet we can get the record of their marriage. And that will give us her maiden name."

Jill had picked up the notebook that shop employees used to record phone calls. She had turned to a blank page and was writing swiftly on it.

Betsy said, "Another thing the Nowickis can tell us is if both the Farmers attended the sale. One of the rumors going around up there is that he deserted the Army, then told her where he was so she could join him. If it turns out the two of them were there to sign the sale papers, that will destroy that rumor."

"He'd have to be there anyway, wouldn't he?" asked Jill. "Lars and I are both on the deed to the cabin, so we both had to sign our names. Major Farmer put Helga's name on the deed with his, so I don't think she could sell it alone."

"If they both had to be there," said Godwin, "that already spoils that rumor, doesn't it?"

But Betsy said, "Power of attorney. If he was in the military, especially if he was going overseas, he might've given her a power of attorney so she could handle things while he was gone. I remember back when I was in the service how now and then there'd be a case of a sailor going on a seven-month cruise, and while he was gone, his wife would clean out their bank accounts, sell the house, and be long gone before he got back home."

Jill's eyebrows rose. "Nice of her."

"Well . . . I know one case where he'd been asking for it the whole three years they were married. She sold everything, his guns, his truck, even his dog. That *was* mean, selling his dog."

"Something else we'll want to make sure of: the order of all this happening. It's possible Dieter lived in the woods until it got too cold and then found this empty cabin to live in."

Betsy struck her forehead with the heel of her hand. "Jill, you are a genius! Sure, think about it: Helga and the major sell the cabin and go off into the sunset, and Dieter finds this empty cabin to hang out in safe from the cold."

Jill nodded. "Maybe it went like this: Major Farmer gets his orders and decides he doesn't want to go into battle. He writes his wife to sell the cabin, which she does. Then he takes a thirty-day leave and turns up in time to sign the papers with her. That gave them a twenty-nine-day head start to disappear. Soon after, Dieter decides he just can't take POW life anymore and walks away. He hides out in the woods for a few weeks, then there's a hard frost and he needs some shelter. He finds the cabin, empty. So see, the Farmers could've been long gone before Dieter found the cabin."

Godwin asked, "Then who murdered him?"

Betsy said, "Maybe some other tramp who had already taken possession?"

Jill said, "Maybe the Nowickis, coming to get the place ready for the winter. They came in and surprised a stranger, who attacked them, and they killed him in a fight. They, being new in the neighborhood, didn't know about the German POW camp, and by the time they found out, they'd already hidden the body and laid the new linoleum down to hide the trapdoor."

"You'd think they'd've figured it out from the big *PW* letters on his clothing."

"If he'd been hiding out for weeks, he'd probably stolen clothing from clotheslines," said Jill.

"Gosh, clotheslines," said Godwin, who had a peculiar fondness for old, once-ordinary things.

"Mama, what's a clothesline?" asked Emma Beth. She held up a limp piece of plastic. "I finished popping."

"It's a thin piece of rope strung up so you can hang wet clothes on it to dry."

"Oh." Emma Beth found this information peculiar but didn't know quite where to go with it.

Betsy took the plastic from the child. "Wow, you did a super job! Thank you!"

"You're welcome," said Emma Beth. "Airey's not finished yet."

Jill said, "Well, we can't wait any longer. Go get him. We need to get going."

"Yes, Mama." She walked off.

"I wonder if we can find out from the pattern when that linoleum was laid. Boy, is there a lot we don't know, to have so many theories about what really might've happened," said Betsy.

"Then I'd better get busy," said Jill.

After she and the children left, Godwin said, "Interesting how she's gotten so keen on sleuthing."

"Yes. I wonder if Lars knows about it."

A BOUT nine o'clock that evening, Betsy took a bottle of her favorite wine and two glasses and went knocking on Connor's door. He was home.

Eleven

IT was getting on for bedtime. Jill was putting the last few stitches in some counted cross-stitch pattern she'd worked up with her usual speed and efficiency. Lars came to look over her shoulder at it.

"Nice," he said.

"You sound like Airey."

"Sorry. But it is nice." He hesitated, then said, "Can I talk with you about something?"

She immediately put her needlework down. "Sure. What is it?"

"Are you serious about going sleuthing with Betsy?"

"Yes, I am. Why?"

"I'm wondering if you're thinking of this as going back on the cops kind of sideways," he said, using cop lingo.

"No, I don't want to go back on the cops. At least I don't think so. Not right now."

"So what is this about?"

"I'm not sure. For once in my life, I'm going strictly on my feelings. And I feel like I need to do this."

"Do you feel like you've outgrown raising the kids?"

"No, of course not. They're my number one priority, my pride and pleasure. It's just that here is our very own mystery. Our own skeleton in the cellar of our own cabin. I'm fascinated by it. I want to know how he came to be down there. I'm so glad Betsy is at least interested—and that she's willing to let me help. And I'm actually of use to her. I never thought I had a head for investigations, but now I think maybe I do."

"So if you do go back on the cops, you'll apply for Mike Malloy's job?"

"I told you, I don't want to go back on the cops."

"So what then, private eye?"

"Maybe," she said. But he had a feeling that's exactly what she was thinking.

But the next few days showed Jill how frustrating sleuthing could be. There were two other families with the surname Ferguson in Cass County—but neither was related to Harlan Ferguson, who had sold the cabin to Matthew Farmer. The neighbors around the Larson cabin had bought their cabins long after World War II, and knew nothing about the Farmers. Betsy had no more suggestions about where Jill should look.

Then came a break, and Jill called Betsy. "I found the Nowickis," she announced.

"The *right* Nowickis?" asked Betsy.

"Yes, one of them is the grandson of the couple that

bought the cabin from the Farmers. They're both dead—the couple who bought it are dead, I mean. Murder-suicide."

"Uh-oh. When did that happen?"

"Nineteen sixty-five, the year the cabin was sold to Buster Martin."

"That's a long time after Dieter Keitel's body was hidden in the root cellar. Any idea what brought it on? Was one of them terminally ill, for example?"

"I don't know. I just found the story in the back editions of the *Star Tribune*. It was a short article. There was no mention of one of them being sick, or a record of domestic abuse. I found their son first, and he refused to answer any questions. Then I talked with the grandson briefly and while he seemed standoffish, he agreed that he would talk with me or with the both of us day after tomorrow. His name is Robert and he lives in Morris."

"Where is Morris?"

"About three hours west of here, almost to the South Dakota border."

Betsy groaned softly, and Jill said, "Hold on, there's good news. He's coming here. He's got some appointments in the Twin Cities, to interview nursing home managers on behalf of his mother-in-law. He says he'll stay over so we can talk with him, if we'll either put him up or pay for his hotel room. There's something wrong about him, about the way he talks about his grandparents."

"Small wonder, considering."

"No, it's not just the way they died. He sounded more angry than sad—even after all those years."

"Ah. Then definitely a motel," said Betsy.

"I agree. I'll split the charge with you, but pick something inexpensive."

"How about the Hilltop? It's right on the edge of town and it's clean." That was about the best that could be said for it. "Or did he sound like the kind of person who would expect to stay at the Hilton?"

Jill smiled. "No, I don't think so. I mean, I'm sure he'd like to, but then so would I. I don't think it's necessary to put him up in first-class accommodations."

But Betsy said, "Still, let's have him stay at The Birdhouse Inn, all right?" The Birdhouse was Excelsior's one remaining bed-and-breakfast; the other, Christopher Inn, had been sold to a developer, who made it part of a big condo complex.

"All right," agreed Jill. It cost more than the Hilltop, but was far nicer. "Where shall we meet to talk with him?"

"How about we take him to dinner? I read somewhere that people are friendlier over a shared meal. Is Patisserie Margo open in the evening?" The Patisserie was new in town, offering homemade soups, muffins, breads, and croissant sandwiches. The croissants were huge and thick, with a dark and flaky surface; Jill and Betsy both loved them. Since the town bakery had closed, the Patisserie was particularly welcome. Plus, it was just two blocks from The Birdhouse.

"No, right now they're only open for lunch. How about Ming Wok? Everyone likes Chinese." It was four blocks from the inn.

"Fine with me."

"I hope Robert can tell us something about the cabin," said Betsy.

"I'm sure his parents took him to it while he was growing up. And told him stories about it—maybe about how their parents came to buy it. That would be useful to us."

GODWIN came in to work the next morning very down. He slouched through the opening up operation, hardly saying anything. Betsy finally asked, "What's the problem, Goddy?" expecting to hear of a quarrel with Rafael.

But Godwin said in a voice of doom, "Golf."

"But you like golf!"

"Not anymore. I've developed a *slice*. No matter what I do, *zoom*!" He gestured forward then off to one side. "The ball goes sailing off to the right. I spent half of my game yesterday playing the ball from the rough and *twice* on the *next fairway over*." He bowed his head, and his lower lip actually trembled. "It was very embarrassing, and Rafael laughed at me," he concluded in a low voice.

With an effort, Betsy kept from laughing, too. "Poor Goddy," she said then, with real compassion, and came to put an arm around his waist.

He turned and hugged her, wetting her shoulder with his tears. "Oh, what am I to *do*?" he sobbed. "I—I love him, and I even love his silly, stupid game, and I'm so *bad* at it!"

"There, there," she said, hugging him back. "You'll get better, you know you will. Isn't Rafael a good teacher?"

"Yes, of *course* he is! The *best*! He's so kind, and so, so *patient* with me." When upset, Godwin used a lot of italics.

"That's right, you told me about that. Was he impatient yesterday?"

119

"No, *of course* not—at least, not that I could *tell*. But he *must* be! I'm so slow and stupid about this *wretched* game, I don't understand it, I just don't *get* it! I was doing so *well* just last week!"

"How long has Rafael been playing?"

"Oh, his father started taking him golfing when he was about *four*! He's been good at it for so long, I don't think he remembers being bad at it! So what am I going to *do*? I was such an *embarrassment* yesterday! I think I should just *quit*!"

Betsy stepped back and took Godwin by the shoulders. "And then what will you do on sunny afternoons when Rafael is out on the course? Or will you try to get him to quit, too?"

"Oh, I would *never* try to get him to quit! Golfing is *too important* to him!" Godwin thought. "I don't know what I'd do. They won't let people who aren't golfing on the course, so I couldn't just follow him around."

Betsy smiled. "You wouldn't like that anyway. By the third hole you'd be begging to borrow a driver and hit just one ball, just once. And when it went sailing down the fairway, straight and true, you'd kick yourself for not bringing your clubs along."

Godwin nodded, and a smile started forming on his lips. "You're probably right. *Especially* if it went sailing straight and true."

"And of course it would, that's the perverse nature of golf." Betsy had never played, but she was sure that was right, because it was true of a lot of things.

Godwin laughed bitterly. "That's just exactly what it would do."

"So don't quit. Try to figure out why your drive is hooking—"

"Slicing."

"Slicing, or listen to Rafael tell you what you're doing wrong, and fix it. Maybe before you go out with him again, go to a driving range, and hit a couple of hundred balls to see if you can get it fixed before you play again."

Godwin nodded. "That's a good idea." He cocked his head at her. "You always give me such good advice. Maybe you should listen to yourself next time you and Connor have a quarrel."

"I'd rather listen to you. My advice to myself is unreliable while your advice is always excellent."

A few minutes later, Betsy heard him whistling a show tune while straightening up the mess a customer had left in a bin of patterns.

Less than an hour later, Jill called. "Good news. I've got a new lead. Remember the old Cass County sheriff, who kept a record of the search for Dieter?"

"Yes?"

"He kept records of the POW camp at Remer, too. And I've got permission to come up and look at them."

"What do you think you might find?"

"Probably nothing. But who knows? I'm just going up for a look."

"When?"

"Right away, today."

"Wait a minute, what about that interview with Mr. Nowicki?"

"You do it, you're better than I am at talking with strangers."

Aaaack, thought Betsy. But she asked, "Are you taking the children?"

"No, they're spending today and tomorrow with their Ganfer Erik and Gram Elise."

Betsy managed not to show her relief at not being asked to baby-sit; she had taken the children one time while in the shop, and found that work was incompatible with two small, rambunctious children. But she promised herself that she'd make up for it pretty soon by taking them for a day. Or an afternoon anyhow.

Betsy was doing bookkeeping that evening when Jill phoned, and in as close to an excited tone as she ever got said, "I'm back—and guess what? She worked at the camp."

"Who—oh, Helga did? That's amazing! What did she do out there?"

"Secretary to the commandant—who was a lieutenant. You know there were nearly five hundred POWs in that camp? Guarded by a handful of soldiers. Must've been an interesting job watching them mill around the exercise yard, driving them out to the forest to cut down trees every morning and picking them up at sunset, counting the knives in the kitchen to make sure they didn't steal one after peeling the potatoes. But much, much better than dodging bullets while slogging through the mud toward Berlin."

"You're in a funny mood."

"There's a book about the POW camps called *Swords into Plowshares*. I found it at the Hennepin County Library at Ridgedale. Reading it puts me so strongly back in that time that I have to remind myself that I'm living in the second decade of the twenty-first century, not in the 1940s."

"I've had books do that to me, but generally they're novels. Anyway, what about Helga?"

"That's all I could find. She worked at the Remer camp as a secretary—probably an administrative assistant, really, if the lieutenant was grass-green, which he was. The sheriff wrote a single word after his name: *Shavetail*, which means new at his job. New at being in the Army, too, more than likely. Probably some grizzled old sergeant really ran the camp—actually, some of the camps did have noncoms in charge."

"Did the information you found give her age? Her date of birth?"

"No, nothing helpful at all. Just her social security number."

"Why her social security number?"

"Beats me. But all the civilian employees, all four of them, had their social security numbers given. Maybe it was a way to make sure they were citizens."

"Can we find something out about her using that?" asked Betsy.

"I don't know what."

"Well, did you find out anything else useful?"

"Both those linoleum patterns were sold for years and years, from about 1938 to 1960, so there's no joy for us there."

"Uff da. Anything else?"

"I think our cabin used to have two bedrooms and no bath—that part we should have deduced from the outhouse."

"How did you find that out?"

"I was driving back and decided to take a quick detour to

our cabin, just for a look, you know, to see if it had burned down or something, and so long as I was in the neighborhood, I went for a look at the one down the way—it's for sale, you know. The real estate agent was there, so I stopped in. That one is in its original configuration, according to the agent. Two bedrooms, a back porch, and an outhouse."

"Is that a negative or a positive fact?"

"I'm not sure when ours was remodeled, so probably another negative."

"Anything else?"

"The investigator up in the Cass County Sheriff's Department has gone through that old sheriff's file, too. He's thinking he's established a link between Helga and Dieter. What do you think?"

"Well, it's probable the POWs knew about the camp commandant's secretary. But I can't see how Helga would know Dieter, unless he was the sort always in the commandant's office about something. And even if he was, why would she tell him where she lived?"

"He probably wouldn't be in there much anyway. I mean, he wouldn't be the spokesman for the POWs, he was just a corporal, and a teenager."

"Maybe he was a troublemaker, always being called in for a scolding or some kind of punishment. Though," added Betsy thoughtfully, "if I were thinking about an escape, I wouldn't be calling attention to myself beforehand. I'd want those guards to think I was just another cowed prisoner and not pay any special attention to me."

"Hmmmm," said Jill. "Maybe. Or maybe the running off

was the final event in an escalating series of misbehaviors and punishments. You know, 'That does it, I'm out of here!' "

Betsy chuckled. "That sounds very plausible. Say, Jill, I had another idea. Do you know how to contact the bear lady, what's her name, Molly something?"

"Fabrae. No, Lars gave her his card with the Cass County Sheriff's Department number on the back of it, but she didn't give us a card in return."

"But she was interested in seeing the cabin, and she knew it was the last place her father lived before he disappeared. I wonder what else she knows?"

"That's easy to find out. Go to Anywho-dot-com and enter her name. She said she's from Saint Paul, didn't she? Fabrae isn't a common name, maybe you'll find a phone number. Then you can ask her."

"All right, I'll try that. You know what else I'd like to try? I'd like to go back up there myself and talk to that little group of old men at The Lone Wolf. If the major's disappearance was a big item of gossip, I bet they'll remember it. And I'll bet they'll remember other things about the Farmers, too."

"Durn," said Jill.

"What?"

"I wish you'd said something about that before I went up there. I could have done that myself."

"Oh, don't worry about it, I think I've been looking for an excuse to go back up. Those men gather for morning coffee, so I'll have to go up the night before. May I stay at your cabin? I want to listen to the loons some more. I'll look at my schedule and call you back about when I can get away."

"Of course you can stay at our place."

"Thank you. Now, don't forget this evening at six we meet at the Ming Wok."

"I won't."

After they hung up, Betsy went to the Anywho web site and inquired about Molly Fabrae. There was no Molly or Mary or M. Fabrae, but there was a John Fabrae and a Henry Fabrae.

She dialed John's number and discovered he was Molly's son. Henry was his father. Betsy thanked him and called Henry.

"Yes, she's right here," he said, and in a moment Betsy heard Molly's voice.

"Hello, *who* is this?" she asked politely.

"My name is Betsy Devonshire. I'm a friend of the Larsons, who bought that old log cabin up on Thunder Lake."

"Oh, yes. What can I do for you?"

"Jill and I have decided to do some poking around to see if we can find out what happened to bring that unfortunate young German prisoner to the root cellar of the cabin."

"Wow, you are? How interesting. But why tell me—Oh, but wait, I'm sure my father had nothing to do with it."

"I'm sure you're right," Betsy lied. "What we're trying to do right now is locate Helga, and I'm hoping you can help."

"How could I help? I never met the woman."

"Do you know anything about her? Her maiden name, for example."

There was a silence that went on so long Betsy began to wonder if the connection had been lost. "Fon," said Molly suddenly.

"I beg your pardon?"

"It was Fon something. Like Fon Schultz or Fon Hindenberg, only neither one of those."

"You mean 'von'?"

"Dad pronounced it 'fon.' Is there a difference?"

"No. 'Fon' is the German pronunciation of a word spelled V-O-N. It means 'from' or 'of.' That's interesting. Can you think of anything else?"

"She was a lot younger than my father. A lot. Years younger."

"Very good. Anything else?"

"Not offhand. I wasn't interested in her, of course. But give me your phone number; if I think of anything else, I'll call you."

"Thank you," Betsy said and complied, adding also her e-mail address. *Good*, she thought as she hung up. *Maybe she can come up with something even more useful.*

Twelve

❖ ❖ ❖

JILL and Betsy met at ten minutes to six outside the Ming Wok restaurant. The air around them was saturated with the scents of hot garlic and brown sauce. Despite her misgivings about the meeting with Robert Nowicki, Betsy yearned to get inside and research the menu. Her mouth was watering.

Jill asked, "Want to play 'good cop, bad cop'?"

"I don't know how to play that."

"Then you be the good cop, all softhearted innocence and willing to believe anything he tells you."

Betsy nodded. "All right. And you will be?"

"Tired of people lying to me."

"What if he doesn't need to be played?"

"All subjects of an interview need to be played."

Betsy nodded. "And this sort of thing works?"

"Surprisingly often, especially on people who haven't

been questioned by the police before. In fact, his reaction to it will tell us whether or not he's been through it before."

"And if he has?"

"Then the jig is up and we play it by ear."

Betsy nodded. Her own method of interviewing people was very much playing it by ear.

They went into the restaurant, which was small, only a dozen tables, with walls of Chinese orange and imitation bamboo paper. The tables had white tablecloths with white paper covers and black lacquer chairs. In here, the scents were even more delectable to Betsy, who had had a cup of soup for lunch and no customary midafternoon snack.

The place wasn't crowded and soon they were seated across from each other near the rear with two maroon plastic pots of hot water and an oval basket full of tea bags in front of them. Betsy picked the jasmine tea, Jill the green tea to sustain them until Robert Nowicki arrived.

He came in about ten after six, a tall, dark man with thick brown hair, a long knobby nose, and large bony fingers. He didn't look nervous; rather, his jaw was set in determined lines, and his lips were pulled thin. Betsy's heart sank when Jill murmured, "That's him."

Jill stood and waved to draw his attention, and he strode over. He was wearing a pale blue dress shirt without a tie, summer-weight trousers, and heavy, dark sandals.

He stood by their table a few moments, his dark eyes moving swiftly between the two women, taking their measure. He looked to be in his late thirties or early forties. "I'm Robert Nowicki," he said in a deep voice. "Which one of you is Jill Larson?"

"I am," said Jill in a crisp tone. "This is Betsy Devonshire, my partner in this business."

"How do you do, Ms. Larson, Ms. Devonshire. What business? I'm hoping one of you can explain what this is about."

"Certainly," said Betsy kindly. "But why don't you sit down? Would you care for some tea? I'm trying to stave off hunger pains with it."

Nowicki suddenly smiled, and his demeanor became pleasant. "Thank you. I guess I could try the tea. I'm sorry if I was rude just now; I've had a rough day. My grandmother-in-law needs to go into a nursing home, though she doesn't think so, and I've been trying to find one that doesn't scare me into agreeing she can stay in her home awhile longer."

"I understand that can be a very tough job," said Betsy, pouring tea from her pot into a cup for him and pushing over the tea caddy. "I'm sorry you're facing it."

Jill pointedly picked up her menu and the other two obediently followed suit. When the waitress, who introduced herself as Annika, and who looked very Scandinavian, came by a minute later, they placed their orders, then Nowicki said, "Now, why did you want to talk with me?"

Jill said, "My husband and I bought a cabin up on Thunder Lake in Cass County and while cleaning it out, we found a human skeleton in the root cellar."

Nowicki stared at her. "That must have been a terrible shock." When she didn't continue, he said, "Is that supposed to be the reason?"

"The cabin used to be owned by Arnold and Marsha Nowicki."

He slowly paled. "My grandparents? Well, I'll be damned."

He tried for a chuckle, which failed. "You mean that old log cabin they used to own? Yes, that's right, it was on Thunder Lake." He frowned and sipped his tea. "I'd almost forgotten about it. My parents said it always smelled in there. Mildew, I think they—But you think . . ." He wiped his mouth with his fingers. "Oh, my God, is it possible . . . ?"

"Is it possible what, Mr. Nowicki?" asked Jill, looking every inch a cop.

"That skeleton was there when they spent their summer vacations up there? No, wait a minute, there wasn't a root cellar in that place, they never said anything about a root cellar. You must have the wrong cabin, you have to mean some other cabin. Besides, I'm sure they would have looked down there. So it can't be their cabin." But his expression remained horrified. "Right?"

"Nossir," said Jill, "it *is* your grandparents' cabin. Your grandparents' name appears on the list of previous owners. They bought it from Helga and Matthew Farmer in 1945, and sold it to Harry Martin in 1965."

Nowicki shook his head slowly, closing his eyes, but more in wishful denial than in disbelief. "This is hard to take in," he muttered. "A horrible thing, to think someone lay—And they didn't—" Then his eyes snapped open. "So why did you want to talk to me?" he demanded. "Just to make me feel bad? It's not my fault there was a skeleton in the root cellar! I never saw the place; I wasn't even born when they owned it!"

"Hold on, hold on," said Betsy placatingly. "We're not accusing you of anything. Please, if you don't mind, just answer a couple of questions, all right?"

Somewhat mollified, he said grudgingly, "All right."

"Now, let's go back to the beginning. Do you know how your grandparents came to buy the cabin in the first place?"

Now Nowicki started to look uncomfortable. "I'm the baby of the family, a real tail-ender," he said after a few moments. "I have an older sister and brother who actually got to meet them. My grandparents were gone before I was born, so everything I know about them is second and third hand."

"That's all right, we'll take that into consideration," said Betsy. "What do you know about them?"

"Well, the family opinion of them isn't good. They were cranky and difficult, to start with. And according to my Uncle Max, Grandfather was something of a crook. During the war he helped people beat the rationing laws, getting beef and sugar and lard from somewhere and selling it without collecting ration book 'points' for them. I don't know how it was done, Uncle Max didn't say."

"Did your grandfather own a farm?" asked Betsy.

"No. He had a house on the edge of town with some land around it, but it wasn't a farm." Nowicki sighed. "He was a ripe old bastard, excuse my language, but that's what Uncle Max used to say. Uncle Max had a crooked face and said it was because his dad, who used to beat him regularly, one time smashed him in the face so hard he broke his cheekbone."

"That's terrible!" said Betsy, shocked.

"What else did he say about him?" asked Jill.

"Not much."

But his tone was so evasive Betsy was emboldened to ask, "Something else, though, isn't there?"

"Well . . . He was hard on all the kids. So hard one of them ran away." Nowicki looked over at the big impressionist painting of bamboo stalks and cherry blossoms on the wall. He added softly, "Or that's what he told the kids, that Uncle Jerry ran away. Jerry was sixteen." He looked at Betsy. "Now you two come along and say there was a skeleton in the root cellar."

Betsy looked thoughtful, but Jill said, "No, we think that skeleton predated your grandparents' ownership of the cabin."

"How do you know that?" He looked at once startled and hopeful.

Betsy said, "The police say the skeleton is that of a man who was a German prisoner of war who walked away from a camp of them up in Remer back in 1944. His ID tag was found with his bones."

"A German POW? In Minnesota? Oh, wait, yeah, I learned about them in high school. There were POW camps all over the U.S. Thousands of Germans were in them. Kind of an incredible thought." He looked like a man reminded of a startling fact he had somehow forgotten.

"Yes, it is."

"And now you say one of them was put into a root cellar and no one knew about it until now."

"That's right," said Betsy.

Jill said, "He was one of the few who walked away, and he was never caught, except by person or persons unknown, who murdered him by fracturing his skull and tossing his body into a root cellar."

"Maybe he fell," said Nowicki. "Heard the owners coming back and he was trying to hide."

"We have good reason to think that isn't the case," said Jill.

"And you say all this happened in 1944," he said.

"Yes," said Betsy.

"But my grandparents didn't own the cabin until 1945, right?"

"Yes," admitted Betsy.

On her admission, Nowicki's volatile nervousness smoothed down. "Well, then, we're back to my first question, what does this have to do with me?"

"We're trying to learn more about the owners back then, Helga and Matthew Farmer. We were hoping you knew some stories about how your grandparents came to buy the cabin, and what might have transpired during the transaction."

"Wow, did you come to the wrong person." He smiled. "I'm sorry, I really am. Especially since you're paying for me to stay the night in this nice little town." He looked around the room, then back at them.

Betsy asked, "Do you think we might persuade someone else, your Uncle Max, say, to talk to us?"

"Probably not." He shook his head.

"If he did," said Jill, "what would he say about his mother?"

"That she backed her husband up in everything he did."

The waitress walked up then with a big round tray holding their food: chicken in hot garlic sauce, beef with ginger scallions, and shrimp with sa dae sauce. All talk came to an end while it was distributed, and they took a few first bites.

Nowicki didn't eat for a few moments, then took a deep

breath and resolutely took a big forkful. "Tastes good," he said, though Betsy was of the opinion that he wouldn't have known if it was good or not, upset as he was by the topic of their questioning.

"What now?" he asked.

"We'll share what you told us with the investigation team up in Cass County," said Jill. "They may come to you and the rest of your family with some questions."

"I'll just bet they do," said Nowicki. "And I wish them luck getting any information out of my folks."

"Where was your grandparents' house, which you said was on the edge of town?" asked Betsy. "I mean, was it in Morris?"

"No, it was in Albert Lea. To this day no one in my family will visit Albert Lea, or even stop for gas there. They wouldn't tell me why until I was in high school. I used to think there were bad people living there."

Jill said, "Just out of curiosity, that murder-suicide: what was that about?"

"Nobody knows. Grandmother shot Grandfather, then herself. No one knows why. What's your interest in this anyhow? Why not just let the cops handle it?"

Jill said, "Much as we admire the police, we are taking a personal interest. It's our cabin, and we want to know why there was a skeleton in the cellar."

Nowicki grimaced. "I guess finding it must have been unpleasant."

"Scary and aggravating," said Betsy. "The police treated the cabin like a crime scene and ran us off while they investigated." When he looked questioningly at her, she said, "I was there, too." She gestured with her fork—she had never mastered the art of eating with chopsticks. "I'm godmother of her daughter."

Now that Nowicki was sure he had nothing more to tell them, he relaxed and the rest of the meal was taken up by pleasant, unhelpful conversation.

I T was a member of the Monday Bunch who suggested a use for the social security number. The next morning, Phil came in to buy yarn to crochet a second cup cover, this one for his wife, and Godwin filled him in on the latest in Betsy and Jill's sleuthing.

"Did you know," said Phil, "that if you send three dollars to the Social Security Administration along with a name and social security number, they will forward a message to that person?"

Betsy chuckled. "Now, Phil, that's *got* to be an urban legend!"

"Swear to God," said Phil, raising both hands and his skein of yarn, right hand higher than the left. "Daughter of a friend of mine reconnected with an old boyfriend that way."

"How did this woman just happen to know her old boy-friend's social security number?"

"Because he had been a soldier, and the Army started using social security numbers as ID numbers and the two of them had written to one another after he joined up. You know, love letters. So she kept them, and his return address had his social security number on it."

"Awwwwww," sighed Godwin. "Did they find out they were still in love?"

"Yeah, but it didn't last. They'd gotten too different from each other. Nothing in common but that long-ago romance."

"Awwww!" said Godwin again but this time his tone was disappointed.

"And you know the daughter?"

"Not personally, but like I said, she's the daughter of a friend of mine. He told me the sad story over a couple of beers one night."

"Fair enough. Three dollars, you say."

"Yes," said Phil with a nod. "You send it to the Social Security Administration. Put your message in an envelope with the person's name and number on the outside. They'll forward it, but it's up to the person to decide whether to get in touch, or not."

"Are you going to try it?" asked Godwin after Phil had left.

"I think I'll let Jill try to contact Helga—those two have the cabin in common, so I think Helga is more likely to respond to Jill."

It was near closing time. Betsy and Godwin were sitting at the library table in the center of the shop talking about the fall window display.

"To keep on with the classes theme, let's put up samplers and schoolhouse patterns," Betsy said. "Which reminds me, I've never worked a sampler. Maybe I should, just to keep things fair."

"'Keep things fair'?"

"Every so often I'll get a customer asking about doing her first sampler. I feel a little awkward recommending one or another when I've never even tried one myself. I should, since they were originally meant to teach little girls various stitches and their alphabet and numbers."

"That's all you need to know about samplers," said Godwin. "The rest is a matter of the stitcher's personal taste. We've got four sampler models on our wall in back, two books, and probably a dozen more patterns to choose from."

"Okay, you're right. The reason I've never stitched a sampler is that I just can't whomp up the desire to."

"One of these days a pattern will come in and you'll jump on it—" The door sounded its two notes, indicating a customer coming in. "Trust me," Godwin concluded, standing to go greet their visitor.

Betsy didn't recognize the customer. She was medium-tall, with brown eyes and hair dyed an attractive streaky brown, wearing a long blue denim dress, matching sneakers, and carrying a purse that looked to be made from an old pair of jeans. She was probably in her middle or late sixties.

"May I help you find something?" Godwin asked.

"I'm looking for Betsy Devonshire," the woman replied, her eyes wandering to and past Betsy, still sitting at the table writing a note on the window planning sheet.

Betsy looked up. "I'm Betsy Devonshire," she said, rising.

"I'm Molly Fabrae."

"Oh, hi! I didn't recognize you! What brings you all the way over to this end of the Cities?"

"I didn't recognize you, either. I'm here because I simply couldn't wait for you to call me. I had to come and talk to you, to see if you've found out anything."

Godwin stepped away from the woman's line of sight, and studied her sharply. Betsy had told him about Molly's conversation with her and Jill.

Now the woman turned a little to look at Godwin, who suddenly developed an interest in checking the display of metallic floss on a nearby spinner rack. Then she looked back at Betsy, an unspoken request twined in her eyebrows.

"Here," said Betsy, "let's go in back where we can sit down and talk a little more privately. Would you like a cup of coffee or tea?"

"A cup of tea would be heaven."

"I have orange pekoe, English breakfast, and several herbals," Betsy said, thereby warning that the teas came in a bag. Some preferred their tea properly prepared from loose leaves.

"Orange pekoe, thank you. No sweetener or lemon, please."

Betsy selected two pretty porcelain cups, poured simmering water from the electric kettle, and brought the beverages to the table—she had chosen for herself a raspberry-flavored herbal tea.

"I don't understand," said Molly after taking a grateful sip. "Is this your store?"

"Yes. What don't you understand?"

"Do you have two jobs, then? Shop owner and private detective?"

"I investigate as an amateur. It's more like a hobby. A serious, driven hobby, but one I don't get paid for."

"Have you been doing it long?"

"A few years. I've met with some success. The local police

department thinks I can be useful at times." Betsy smiled, remembering the days when Sergeant Mike Malloy had considered her a hazardous interference with his job.

"What are you trying to accomplish in the case of the old cabin?"

"I'm assisting Jill Larson. Her husband is a police sergeant and she's a former police sergeant who quit to raise their children. More than her husband, I think she's taking it personally that a vacation home they brought their children to turns out to have had a human skeleton in the cellar. She wants to know, 'All right, who put that there?' A very typical cop attitude, if you think about it."

Molly choked on her tea as a little laugh was forced from her. "I would think of it more as a mommy attitude myself. Okay, I understand where she is coming from, but how do you figure in?"

"Jill is among my very closest friends. She has asked me to assist her, and I've agreed."

"And you're looking for Helga fon-what's-her-name Farmer."

"And her husband, your father. You said he disappeared?"

"Yes." Molly frowned at her father being brought into the discussion, but then she nodded. "All right, let me tell you about him. He got orders overseas, and before he was to board the transport ship, he got leave to come home—to his home with Helga, that is—and arrange things—you know, make sure the insurance was paid up, the house was in good order, like that."

Betsy nodded. "Where were they living?"

"In the cabin. Helga was from up there. I think she may have had family up there. The war had started and he was going to be away a lot, so he wanted her to be near her family. But it took him away from his original family, me and my mother and my two brothers." She paused. "Well, Billy, he was the older one, enlisted in the Army as soon as he turned seventeen, which was in 1942—and then we lost him. Billy died in a car accident in England just two months out of boot camp."

"I'm so sorry," said Betsy, speaking to the pain in Molly's eyes.

"Thank you. And then the Army came by again, this time looking for Dad. I don't remember any of this—it's funny the things you remember and don't from when you're small. I remember a little doll with frizzy hair and the color of the blanket on my bed. What I don't remember is the day the Army came to tell my mother her son was dead or when they came again a year later wondering if she'd heard from Dad because he was supposed to report for duty at the Presidio in San Francisco and never did."

Trying to keep from crying, Molly lifted her eyes and let them wander around the walls of that part of the shop. They were covered with finished models of counted cross-stitch patterns. "This is a nice place," she said.

"Thank you," said Betsy. "That must have been a terrible time for your mother. Is she still living?"

"No, she died twenty years ago. Cancer."

"How sad and awful."

"Yes, it was a long, terrible struggle."

Betsy took a sip of her tea. "I would have liked to talk with her."

"She probably would have told you what she always said to me: 'That woman'—meaning Helga—killed him.'"

"And you think so, too?"

"I guess I do. I mean, when I heard about the skeleton, I thought, Mama was right, she was right. But now they say the skeleton is of some German prisoner who escaped. That doesn't make any sense to me! What would a German prisoner be doing in that cabin? What do you think happened?"

"I don't know. I do know Helga worked at the POW camp in Remer, but how the prisoner knew where she lived, I have no idea. It was probably a coincidence that he ended up in her cabin, though why he came there and who killed him is a mystery. Was he killed because he came there? Or would he have been killed in any case, and it just happened to be there?"

"What are they going to do with the bones?"

"I should think they'll try to find any family he might have in Germany and send his remains back to them for burial."

Molly nodded once, and said bitterly, "Then they, at least, have an old question answered."

"Maybe when we find Helga, she can tell us what happened to your father."

Angry hope flared in Molly's eyes. "That would be wonderful! Do you think you can actually find her?"

"We're trying hard. It's possible, of course, that she's no longer alive. I promise to let you know as soon as we find out something."

Molly finished her tea and left, and Betsy resumed her

seat at the library table with Godwin. They had barely found their places in the patterns and models and sheets of paper on the table when the door again sounded and this time Connor came in.

"Hello, pet," he said just a hair too cheerfully, and Godwin gave Betsy a huge smile.

Betsy smiled back. "Hello, Connor," she said. "What's up?"

"I want to come with you to Thunder Lake," he said.

"Well, you can't," she replied. "I'm going to be very busy."

"Now, Betsy," scolded Godwin mildly, adding to Connor, "Why do you want to go with her?"

"Because I'd like to see her working her 'hobby.' And because I'd like some time alone with her—we haven't had much of that lately."

"And whose fault is that?" asked Betsy, feeling a touch of anger.

"Mine. Entirely mine," he said, so meekly the stone in her heart melted. "Will you forgive me?"

"Yes," she decided. He came to sit in a chair beside her and take her hand.

"Now, isn't that better?" he said, and she immediately released his hand.

"Of course it is," said Godwin. "See how nice it is when you stop being mad at each other? Betsy, I think you should let him come along."

"Please don't be angry with me," said Connor. "I'm doing the best I can, truly."

She looked into his charming, earnest face and sighed. If

only she didn't like him so much! "Very well," she said. "I'm not angry—and yes, you can come along."

WHEN Betsy spoke to her that evening, Jill was surprised and pleased to find there might be a way to contact Helga. "Will you help me write the letter? What kind of a note would she be most likely to respond to?"

Betsy thought for a minute. "I know. 'We bought the pretty little cabin you used to live in. We're thinking of remodeling it. Would you be willing to tell us what it was like when you lived in it?'"

"Yes, that sounds a whole lot like a message that would intrigue her. But would she reply?"

"If I were Helga, I'd want very much to know if someone was about to uncover that trapdoor. Especially since they found out who I am, and maybe even where I live."

Thirteen

❖ ❖ ❖

THEY left late Saturday afternoon after the shop closed. They took Betsy's car because she knew the way.

The terrain didn't change a whole lot. The land was gently rolling, mostly prairie but here and there forests of elm, maple, ash, birch, and every kind of evergreen: white and red pine, juniper, balsam, spruce—even, as they got nearer their destination, the scrubby jack pine. The farther north they went, the more the pines and birch predominated, but the other kinds of trees never disappeared, as they did the time Betsy went with Jill up to the north shore of Lake Superior.

Connor had a comforting ability to sit still and not speak. She was aware of him in the passenger seat, his craggy-handsome profile, the faint scent of his aftershave. Once out of the city, Betsy said, "So, do you think the Beatles or the Rolling Stones had a better band?"

He laughed softly. "I was wondering when you were going to bring that up." As it turned out, Betsy preferred the Beatles, Connor the Stones.

They talked about other things. Betsy, being a small-business owner, was more to the right politically than Connor, but not enough for it to be a deal breaker. Connor was surprised to learn that Betsy knew the words to some old English music hall songs, and they spent a few miles singing, "Where did you get that hat, Where did you get that tile? Isn't it a nobby one and just the proper style? I should like to have one, Just the same as that. Where'er I go, they'd shout, 'Hello! Where did you get that hat!'"

"My father used to sing that," said Betsy. "He told me there was a rumor that Prince Phillip, on seeing Queen Elizabeth wearing her crown for the first time, whispered in her ear, 'Where did you get that hat?'"

Connor laughed—he had a very pleasant laugh. "Sounds just like the old boy. Though of course, when she put on the crown, they were both so young." He fell silent for a few seconds.

Betsy said, "There's an Amish saying, 'We grow too soon old and too late smart.'"

"Yes, indeed. Though some of us never quite get to the latter. Betsy—"

"It's all right, Connor. Really, it is. She's your daughter, after all." She reached out a hand and he took it. His clasp was warm and strong, and she drove for several miles one-handed, loath to let go.

"She'll apologize next time you see her," he promised.

"Don't force anything. I'd hate to be the cause of a breach."

"I don't think that will be the case. I explained to her in words of one syllable or less that I can do as I please with whomever I please."

Betsy smiled. "'I'm Burlington Bertie, I rise at ten-thirty, and saunter along like a toff,'" she warbled. He immediately joined in. "'I'm all airs and graces, correct easy paces, without food so long I've forgot where my face is. I'm Burlington Bertie from Bow!'"

They laughed and then talked about other things they had in common: knitting, live theater, love of horses and old movies, Asian food.

"Say, would you like to learn to golf?" he asked. "I have a feeling I've never really given the game a proper chance."

"No, I don't have time. But if you want to make Goddy happy, talk golf to him. He's still a duffer, but he likes the game—and his friend Rafael is passionate about it."

"About Godwin . . ."

"What about Godwin?"

"I hope you're paying him what he's worth."

"Of course I'm not. I couldn't afford to pay him what he's worth."

"He's very attached to you, too."

"We've seen each other through some tough times."

"I tell you what, when we get married, we'll adopt him."

"What!?"

Betsy suddenly found it difficult to draw a deep breath. She could feel her blood rushing to her face, and her grip on the steering wheel was so hard that her knuckles showed white.

I'm angry; why am I so angry? she thought. She could not

focus on her driving and so she pulled into the next gas station she saw. She stopped the car in a parking area, got out, and went into the store, all without a word.

Connor followed her in a puzzled silence. Betsy bought a bottle of water and paid for it, walked out, and headed for her car. But before she got in, she turned and confronted him.

"How dare you?" she demanded.

"How dare I what?" he asked, smiling as if she were being obtuse about an obvious joke.

"How dare you casually speak of what we'll do after we're married? You don't know if I even want to get married, much less if I want to marry *you*!"

"Do you?"

"Do I what?"

"Want to get married?"

"No, I don't," Betsy replied, not sure if that might be true. But having said it, she realized it was. She even knew why. "My life is good right now, and progressing nicely. I don't need the complication of a husband."

"Couldn't I fit in there *somewhere*?" He seemed a little taken aback.

"Of course you can—and you do. I like you, I like knowing you're right across the hall, that I can come knocking on the door, knowing it's you who will open it. On the other hand, I also like that you're not crowding up my bathroom."

He blinked and then smiled, because she'd said bathroom, not bedroom. "Ah, I see. The old 'I don't want to share a bathroom' syndrome."

"Oddly enough, I think that sums it up nicely." Betsy felt a bit calmer now. She got in the car, opened her bottle of water, and took a drink, letting the cold water cool her heated throat. "Did you ever see *Mr. Blandings Builds His Dream House?*"

He got in beside her, thinking. "Myrna Loy and Cary Grant?"

"That's right. Remember that scene in the tiny apartment bathroom with the two of them trying to shave, comb their hair, and brush their teeth with only one sink between them? I've lived that scene. You're sweet, Connor, but I love being the only one in the bathroom in the morning when I'm trying to get ready for work."

He sighed, faux downcast. "And you didn't think to put two sinks in my bathroom when you remodeled, did you?"

She smiled wryly. "No, I didn't. Sorry." Her anger was totally gone now, replaced by a curious emptiness. Was she wrong to brush him off so strongly? She was honest in saying "not right now," but she did like him. On the other hand, it struck her as cruel of him to make a joke of their still-forming relationship. "We need to be able to go on being friends," she said. "With my track record, I don't dare let myself get close to someone unless we're really good friends first."

"Ah, *machree*," he said in a thick Irish accent, a trick he'd done before, "we'll be friends and all as long as ye can stand it."

They drove for a good mile in a comfortable silence, then he asked, "What's the state of the investigation? What do you know, and what do you hope to find out on this trip?"

Betsy was relieved that the conversation had taken a different turn. "Well, I saw for myself the skeleton in the root cellar of the log cabin that Jill and Lars bought about six weeks ago. We have pretty much decided that it went into the cellar in the form of a German prisoner of war. This was in the late summer of 1944."

"Why 1944?"

"That's the year the young man disappeared, plus it's the date on some jars of canned green beans that were also in the cellar."

"I take it nobody else disappeared up there that year."

"Actually, someone did. The cabin was owned by Helga and Matthew Farmer, and he disappeared a few months after Corporal Keitel did. The Army declared Major Farmer a deserter and he was never found."

"But you don't think the bones are Major Farmer's because—?"

"Because an ID tag with Keitel's name on it was found with the bones. And because the description of Keitel includes a gold tooth and I saw that tooth in the skull with my own eyes." Betsy was suddenly struck by a new thought. "*And* because of the buttons. During the war, everyone in uniform had to wear it all the time—no civilian clothes. But the buttons in the cellar weren't brass; they didn't come off a uniform." She smiled, feeling the warm satisfaction that comes with putting a new clue in place.

"That sounds very convincing. So okay, the skeleton is Corporal Keitel's. What happened to the major?"

"Nobody knows. It's possible he was mugged on the train to Chicago or, more likely, on the train to California and his body was tossed from the train into a lonesome ravine and never found. It's also possible that he was frightened by the possibility of losing his safe stateside job and deserted. There was a rumor—there still is a rumor—that he settled some-where under a new name, sent for Helga, and she joined him after selling the cabin to a family named Nowicki."

"Have you talked to the Nowicki family?"

"Yes, to the one member willing to talk, but he couldn't tell us anything useful. I want to talk to a little group of retired men who have coffee every morning at this old general store called The Lone Wolf, to see if any of them can put me in touch with Helga's family. We've already touched base with a daughter of Matthew Farmer from his first marriage, but all she knows is that Helga was years younger than Matthew. Oh, and when she heard about the skeleton, she thought it was her father, and that Helga had murdered him. She seemed disappointed to learn that that wasn't true."

"That's interesting."

Half an hour later, they pulled up the narrow lane into the clearing in which the log cabin stood. Betsy shut the engine off and they sat for a minute, recovering from the trip and taking in the scene.

"It's like something in a movie," remarked Connor at last. "Very pretty."

"Is there anything like this back home?"

"You mean in Ireland? No, not quite. Oh, there are trees as large as this in great forests, but the landscape is greener and tamer, and has fewer pine trees. And the little cottage would likely be wattle and daub, with a thatched roof." He gave a sigh. "But that's not home, not for me anymore."

"Yet you miss it."

"No. No, I don't. I was a seafaring man starting in my teens and for many, many years, which effectively broke most of my ties to a homeland. Killarney is beautiful, but so is Hong Kong, and Port Elizabeth in South Africa, and New York City." He smiled at her. "So is Duluth, Minnesota—can you tell I love harbor cities? But Lake Minnetonka is very attractive; and Excelsior is a charming little Midwestern town. I'm happy to live here, because someone I'm very fond of lives here, too." He looked at her with those steady dark blue eyes and her heart melted.

"Oh, Connor," she sighed.

"Now come on, friend, show me around."

They put their suitcases in the cabin, and the block of ice they'd bought in Outting into the ice box.

"Very snug," pronounced Connor after Betsy gave him the tour. Looking at the wood-burning kitchen stove, he said, "Do you know, when I was a lad, my gran had a stove like this. She could tell if the oven was the right temperature to bake a pie by thrusting her hand in it for a few seconds. She baked a lovely apple pie."

"I hope you don't expect me to bake a pie in that stove."

"No, but maybe I can try one. Is there a grocery store in the area?"

"That place we're going in the morning for coffee and rolls is the local general store."

Connor smiled approval. "Sounds good."

Betsy decided not to get her hopes up too high for apple pie. Meanwhile, she and Connor explored the rest of the property.

The shed looked very tumbledown, but the roof had kept the rain out and the single window was unbroken. It was infested with spiders and daddy longlegs and other insects, which made them cautious while idling through the stacks of books and old magazines in one corner. There were quite a few ancient editions of the Bobbsey Twins and Hardy Boys among the books, much eaten by insects and chewed by mice. The magazines had been treated equally unkindly, in addition to being yellowed by time.

"Look, these books are pre—World War Two," said Connor, noting how white the remaining pages were. "Paper went to hell during the war." He picked up a magazine devoted to knitting, shook it lightly, and its pages crumbled and fell in a pale yellow avalanche to the dirt floor.

The magazines in the middle of the stack fared better, having been protected from the air. One was on crochet, and Betsy opened it with interest.

"Looking for something?" asked Connor.

"There's a crocheted rug in a chest in the cabin and I hope we can find the instructions in here somewhere. Not in this one, however." She found and paged through several other old survivors. "Oooh, look at this!"

"Find it?"

"No, but look at this darling shawl!"

He looked over her shoulder at the shawl in the magazine, covered with animal figures. "Looks complicated."

"Yes, I'll have to ask Peggy for help with it."

"You're going to bring that magazine back with you?"

"Yes. I'll show it to Jill, of course, but I'm sure she won't mind—she doesn't do crochet."

As the sun settled behind the trees, the air grew chilly and they left the shed and went back to the cabin. There, Connor built a fire in the pot-bellied stove while Betsy lit the kerosene lamps. They made a supper from the cold cuts and hard rolls they'd brought along. By the time they'd finished eating, it was fully dark outside and the lamps made a golden warm glow in the living area.

" 'The light shines in the darkness, and the darkness does not overcome it,' " said Connor.

But Betsy pictured the whole hemisphere of the earth turned away from the sun, facing the immense darkness of space, and the little lamps felt like incredibly frail pinpricks against such an appalling void. " 'O Lord, Thy sea is so great, and my boat is so small,' " she said.

Connor chuckled, surprised. "I've felt that at sea many a time."

"Is it a lonesome occupation?"

"I never thought so, but the crews are small, even on the bigger vessels, so it's helpful if everyone has a talent for getting along. It can be kind of a shock to be at sea with only a dozen other people to talk to for several weeks, then get turned loose in a big city full of tens of thousands of strangers."

"Yes, I can see that."

As they were clearing the card table, there came the big giggle that was the call of the loon.

"My God, they sound just like the recordings!" said Connor, turning to look toward the back of the cabin.

They sat up for a while, talking of inconsequential things; then Connor, whose arm had slipped around Betsy without her noticing it, leaned in and gave her a gentle kiss. She kissed him back, and he kissed her again, more warmly. She felt herself begin to respond and yielded to it.

Before she realized it, they were at it like a pair of teens—

and then she did realize it and it made her chuckle, breaking the mood.

Connor seemed disappointed by her amusement, even when she explained it, but he understood the concept of a broken mood. He set about rebuilding it, tender but insistent and very patient.

Later, Betsy banked the fire while Connor went out for a bucket of water to set on top of the stove to warm for morning.

They went to sleep to the haunting music of the loons.

Fourteen

IN the morning the bucket of water was only a little warmer than the air, but better than the chilled water produced by the pump. Betsy and Connor did minimal ablutions, dressed, and set out for The Lone Wolf. It was a little after eight, but the sun had come up in summer strength, promising a warm day. Betsy wore white linen slacks, a deep-red bell-sleeved blouse ornamented with five large buttons down each sleeve, and sandals. Connor wore faded jeans, a white dress shirt with the sleeves rolled back, and deck shoes. They rode in silence. Connor was not a morning person.

They pulled into the rustic lodge-like building with its moribund gas pumps in front and parked on the gravel apron near the steps. Three cars were already parked there.

The steps led up to a wide deck. A separate entrance off to the right led into a liquor store.

They entered through a creaking screen door and stood

for a moment to allow their eyes to adjust from bright sunlight to the deep-shade interior.

On their left stood the big, old-fashioned bar and at its near end sat five well-seasoned men. Betsy immediately recognized three of them from her last visit, though she hadn't gotten their names. The smallest one, who was also obviously the eldest, recognized her, too.

"Wasn't you in here just a week or so ago?" he asked. "You was with that Larson fellow, bought that cabin they found the skeleton in."

"That's right," said Betsy, stepping forward. "I'm Betsy Devonshire and this is my friend Connor Sullivan."

"Ralph Olson. Grab a stool if you've a mind to. The coffee's terrible but it's better than the water all by itself."

"Now, Ralph," chided a plump old man in a high, rough voice, "don't go bad-mouthing things, or Pat will run us all off." He nodded sideways at the dark-haired young woman behind the bar. "My name's Don Tjerle." He pronounced it "surely." He held out a big, soft hand. Betsy took it and slid onto a vacant stool next to him.

Connor sat down at the end of the group and, with a gesture, ordered a cup of coffee. "Black," he mouthed.

"I take my coffee with all the fixings," stated Betsy.

"So what're they gonna do with them bones?" asked Ralph, after Betsy had doctored her coffee to her satisfaction.

"I don't know, I was hoping you might tell me."

"I heard they're looking for family in Germany to send them home to," said Don. As he spoke, Betsy noted his high cheekbones and curiously slanted light blue eyes—Finn traits.

But *Tjerle* was a Norwegian surname. There were some who would consider him of mixed blood.

"Why do that? Isn't there a cemetery right in Remer?" asked the biggest man, both tall and heavyset. He had small, merry eyes and a short nose under straight, thinning white hair. "You know, where they buried the other POWs." He nodded at Betsy. "Kevin Swanson," he said by way of introduction.

"Nope," said Ralph. "None of the other ones died at that camp, they all made it home safe."

"How do you know so much?" demanded Kevin.

"Some of it I remember," said Ralph. "The rest I read about in a book, which you could do worse than read."

"Ahhhh," growled Kevin. "I don't believe you read any book, I don't believe you know how to read."

"No, it's Donny who doesn't know how to read."

"Never saw any need to learn how," said Don with a small, judicious nod. "I hired a secretary who could read, and I practiced law for thirty years without cracking one law book."

Connor, smiling to himself—he didn't watch the old men plaguing one another—finished the last of his coffee and signaled for a refill. "Have you got anything suitable for breakfast you can sell me?" he asked in a low voice while the young woman refilled his mug.

"Raised donuts," she said. "Fresh this morning. Otherwise there's pairs of hard-boiled eggs back in the chill box."

"Bring me two donuts," said Connor and slid off his stool. "Want a hard-boiled egg, *machree*?" he asked Betsy.

"Yes, please," she replied.

So long as the young woman was there, she went up and around the curve of the bar, refilling mugs. "And I'll have a donut, too, thanks," Betsy said when the woman got to her.

The last man put a big hand over the top of his mug while fishing in his pocket with the other. He pulled out a dollar bill and then two quarters and put the money on the bar. "That does it for me, I'm going fishing," he said and started for the door.

"Hey, Tony!" called Don.

"What?"

"What did I say to make you go away? So I can say it earlier tomorrow."

Tony snorted derisively and went out, letting the screen door slap shut behind him.

Connor came back with two packs of eggs. Betsy took one egg—it was already peeled—and put it on the little plate that held her glazed donut. The donut was tasty, the egg was fresh, and despite the warning, she found the coffee strong without being bitter, and warming to her soul. Even Connor was starting to look more aware of his surroundings.

"Did this place used to be a bar?" he asked halfway through his second egg.

"It was a tavern first," said Ralph. "Man name of John D. Brigham built it, some people still call this place Brigham's. Later, that room where the coolers are got added, and it became a dance hall, then the addition that's a liquor store was put on. During the war, this place had the only phone hereabouts, so Brigham had to take telegraph messages about soldiers killed or missing in action and deliver them. Hated that part of it. He got drafted himself toward the end of the war, even though he was in his middle thirties by then. They took him because he was single." Ralph looked around at the other men, pleased by their attention, then looked at Betsy slantwise. "Take a look at the front door over there."

Betsy and Connor—and the other men, too—turned to look at the open door. It was painted gray and had numerous black, thumbhole-size pock marks in it.

"Those are bullet holes," he said. "Not all of you know Brigham bought it in Chicago and brought it up because the bullet holes was put in it by John Dillinger."

"Is that true?" asked Betsy.

Don said, "It could be. Gangsters were heroes up here in the thirties. They'd come up here when the heat was on back home in Chicago or Saint Paul. You wouldn't believe it today, but this was a great hideout for that kind of man back then."

"That's interesting," said Betsy. "That door story doesn't seem likely, but it's interesting."

"Gangsters liked it up here because it was quiet and the lawmen weren't always poking their noses into everyone's business."

Ralph said, "Did you know it was from up here they got the word *sitting duck*? It comes because commercial hunters used to take a live wild duck and put a collar on it and fasten it to a stool—this is also where they got the expression *stool pigeon*, because they did the same thing with a wild dove— lots of folks couldn't tell the difference between a pigeon and a dove. They'd put the duck out at the edge of a marsh an' when the big flocks go over, the fastened-down duck would call and the others would come in for a landing and get shot.

Or a dove stuck out in a field would call its friends to help. They used to send barrels full of ducks and pigeons and geese to Chicago restaurants."

"Ralph, you are a walking encyclopedia of local history, you know that?" remarked Don.

"Yeah," said Kevin, "but how much of it is true and how much of it is the product of brain fever brought on by underwork?"

"God blame it, it's all true, every word! I got one o' them duck collars at home in my garage. I could show it to you anytime you like, you bet!"

"Oh, yes, I'm sure you could," said Kevin, nodding elaborately. "Right after you finish making it."

Betsy said, "Ralph, since your memory is so good, maybe you can help me with something."

"Probably," said Ralph, sneering at his compatriots, then looking very confidently at Betsy.

"During World War Two, a husband and wife named Matthew and Helga Farmer owned the cabin the Larsons bought. Would you happen to know anything about Helga Farmer? Her maiden name, for example?"

Ralph fell silent for a few moments. Then, "They had a big ol' '36 Auburn convertible she drove while he was away. He was in the Army but stationed somewhere in Wisconsin, I believe. Story we heard told was, he ran off when he got orders to ship out to a war zone. They had Army investigators up here looking for him, a lot of people remember that, you bet. Someone said they saw her kiss him good-bye at the train station and cry as it pulled out for Chicago. What *was* her last name afore she married? She had family around here."

"I heard it was von something," hinted Betsy.

"That's right, it was von Dusen!" shouted Ralph. "There was a whole kit 'n' kaboodle of 'em up here, but they're about all gone now, I betcha. She had three—no, four—no, three brothers and a sister but all that generation is dead or moved away—she was the baby of her family. My mother said they treated her bad and that's why she married that Army fella when she was barely grown up enough. Musta been sixteen or seventeen and her mother and dad wouldn't come to the wedding, my mother told me. Said her brother had to give her away. Her parents had meant her to stay at home and take care of them in their old age. They even took her out of school. But somehow she got this little old part-time job waitressin' and met this Army officer and he just swept her off her feet—or maybe she swept him, she was a really pretty thing, with big blue eyes and blond hair that didn't come from a bottle. I kinda remember her—at least I remember I used to think she was prettier than Betty Grable."

"So there aren't any von Dusens left in the neighborhood?"

"Well, am I a fool or what? Got a memory like a sieve. Yes, there are, or a grandson anyway. You go over by Snowball—"

Kevin interrupted. "There ain't any Snowball, Ralph, you know that."

"Yah, but there used to be and there's still Snowball Lane. Out offa 54, couple-few miles, it's the first tar road on the right past Stoney Creek Road. Look for a church with a red door, it's a mile or two beyond that. The oldest son's grandson's farming it now, name of . . . of Larry. Larry von Dusen. Nice house, white with black trim, and a big red barn. You can't miss it."

* * *

WELL, yes they could. First of all, the county had tarred several of the roads out off 54, and they spent some time wandering up the wrong ones. They thought Snowball Lane wasn't marked, but finally Betsy noticed a street sign—curious to find a street sign out in the country—that had been struck by a vehicle and bent so far over that tall weeds obscured it. Then, the von Dusens had repainted their house cream with red trim. Connor caught the name on the big silver mailbox as they drove by it the second time.

Mrs. von Dusen came to the front door accompanied by the fragrance of fruit pies baking and said her husband was in the barn. They found him by following the mild swear words drifting out of a side room. He was standing amid the ruins of a generator, with a big red multidrawer tool chest beside him.

He was a tall, lean man in his early forties with broad shoulders and big, work-thickened hands heavily stained with grease and rust. He wore the farmer's uniform of blue chambray shirt and overalls, also stained.

A thick head of pale auburn hair topped blond eyebrows and a deep pink complexion. He had a slow, deliberate way of speaking. He was glad to take a break and talk with them.

"I have no memory of her, of course," he said, referring to Helga. "My grandfather said she was beautiful but not very bright. But Great-Aunt Gretchen heard him say that and said she got that Army officer to marry her, didn't she?" Larry smiled at the memory. "She made up a rhyme about it, and it became a family joke. How did it go? I used to speak a little German, but I've forgotten most of it now." In a bad German accent, he said, *"Ein schlaues Madchen wahlt ihren Mann, und lasst sich von ihm jagen, bis sie ihnfangen kann."*

Connor burst into surprised laughter.

"What?" asked Betsy.

"Well, my German's worse than his, but I think what it means is something I've heard Americans say, too: A clever woman lets a man chase her until she catches him."

Betsy made a face—then she grew thoughtful.

Von Dusen nodded. "Yes, that's what it means. The old folks all spoke German, even though they were all born here in Minnesota. Opa and Oma came over from the old country and bought this farm, and considered themselves Americans, but they spoke German at home. The people I call the old folks—my grandfather and his brothers and sisters—didn't speak English till they started school. This is my grandfather's barn—he raised it on the site of the first barn after it burned down in 1924. He was the oldest son, so he got the land and buildings. My father was his oldest son, and I was his only son."

Connor asked, "What was that Army major doing up here anyway?"

"They say he was inspecting the old wood pulp factory that was making cardboard boxes for the Army. I heard she was flirting with his driver before she shifted her attention to him. Bigger game, my grandpa said."

Betsy asked, "Do you know where your Aunt Helga went after she left the cabin over on Thunder Lake?"

"Not an idea in the world."

"Are any of the old folks still alive?"

"No. Uncle Hans was the last to go, and he died ten or eleven years ago."

Connor asked, "Couldn't Helga still be alive?"

Larry bit his under lip while he considered that briefly. "I suppose so," he conceded. "But if she is, she's pretty old, and she's been running awful quiet for a whole lot of years."

"Is it possible one of your cousins hears from her, or knows where she is?"

"No, I'm sure they don't. We had a big family reunion right here on the farm after Uncle Hans died, and Cousin Emily did a family tree showing who was married to who and where they're living and she put a question mark under Great-Aunt Helga's name. She was asking everyone if they knew where she was, and nobody knew. Which is kind of a shame when you think about it. I mean, it's not like she's the black sheep or something. Oma and Opa were mad at her for getting married so young. But you know how it is when you're young, you think you know goddam everything about everything." He gave a big sigh, and Betsy wondered if he didn't have a particular son or daughter of his own with that attitude.

He must have read that in her face because a grin appeared and he nodded. "Yep, I got one like that. Runs in the family, I guess."

"Let's go to Remer for lunch," said Betsy in the car a few minutes later. "I want to see the place where the POW camp was. I wonder what's left of it?" She smiled. "I always was a sucker for ruins."

"Doesn't surprise me. I always thought the reason you liked me is because I'm so old."

"You're not such a relic."

"You're a mere child compared to my antiquity." He burst into song—he had a very pleasant baritone. " 'I was born a hundred thousand years ago, there ain't nuthin' in this world that I don't know, no place that I ain't been, 'round the world and back again, and I'll whup the man who says it isn't so!' "

Betsy laughed. "I wouldn't dream of whupping you. I don't think a whupping would make a lick of difference." They drove in silence for a mile. Then, "How about we go back to the cabin and pack up? We can start for home from Remer."

"Have I offended you again?" He tried for a light tone, but she could hear anxiety in the background of his query.

So it was a pleasure to relieve it. "No, it's just that I think we've gotten nearly everything there is to get from this trip."

In Remer, they entered a little café called The Woodsman. It had big front windows and an entrance that led to a set of four steps going up. Inside was the heavy fragrance of fried food and coffee. The tables were dark wood with paper placemats, and the walls were ornamented with plain-framed photographs of forests that looked taken from calendars.

The waitress was a nice motherly type who recommended the meatloaf.

Questioned, she said she was new to the area and pointed out the family group toward the back. "That's the owner," she said. "He'll probably know all about the old camp."

He didn't, as it turned out—but his wife did. "My grandfather worked out there during the war," she said. "He used to tell stories to us about it, said the prisoners were young and handsome, not bad people—though there was always that ten percent, organizing rallies and trying to push the others around."

"Do you know where the camp is?" asked Connor.

She did.

The directions were easy to follow, but the place they led to was just a large grove of mature pine trees. A nearly overgrown logging trail led into the grove. Betsy pulled off the road and the two got out.

"I wonder if this is the place," said Betsy. "I don't see anything but trees."

"We followed the directions, and they were pretty simple—Route 4 past the rock quarry and the cemetery. Look for the tall pines, she said, and here they are. There's no place like this place anywhere near this place, so this must be the place."

Betsy smiled at the old jest and strode across the road. Stepping into the grove of pines was like going indoors; the harsh sunlight was dimmed and the air turned several degrees cooler. The faded old trail leading in split right inside the grove, one branch going straight ahead and the other off to the right. Underbrush filled the space under the trees, dappled sparsely with green sunlight. A mosquito hummed its high, tight tone in her ear and she slapped at it. There was no sign of human habitation anywhere in sight, only here and there a tree stump covered with moss.

She walked up the straight-ahead trail a hundred yards or so, looking in vain for a tumble of stone foundation, a collapsed clapboard wall, a fallen chimney.

"It's as though it never happened," Connor said at last.

But Betsy remembered the heap of human bones in the root cellar and shivered. That was real. A young German soldier had walked away from this very place and wound up dead in a root cellar less than twenty miles from here. How? And why?

Fifteen

❖ ❖ ❖

A ND there the investigation stalled until Jill phoned Betsy
in her shop a couple of weeks later. "She's dead," Jill
said.

Betsy was in the middle of writing up a sales slip when
the phone rang. "Who's dead?" she said, which startled the
woman buying the fistful of Kreinik silks. Betsy made a reas-
suring gesture at her and continued writing.

Jill said, "Helga Farmer—only she died as Helga Ball. In
New Ulm, by the way. Fifteen years ago."

"Helga Ball—she must have remarried. Divorced her
husband, you think?"

"More likely widowed," said Jill. "Considering the history they shared."

"I wonder if Molly Fabrae knows about this. No, of course
she doesn't, or she would have told us. Did the letter tell you
her husband's name?"

"No, just that she's dead, when she died, and where."

"So what's the next step?"

"I've called up the white pages phone book on my computer and am looking at how many Balls there are in New Ulm."

"And?"

"There are three, a Jean, a Mark, and a Peter. Certainly worth a closer look."

"So let's call them. What story shall we tell? We can't barge in saying we want to ask how a skeleton came to be found in Helga von Dusen–Farmer Ball's cellar."

"No, that wouldn't do." Jill sounded amused.

"I know, we'll say we're doing some genealogy. Larry von Dusen said a cousin did a family tree for a reunion and was wondering what happened to Aunt Helga. You can be a cousin from another side of the family."

"No, you be the cousin. You're a better liar than I am."

"What me, a liar? I prefer actress. But all right. Give me the phone numbers and I'll call."

"No, don't call, we don't want to warn them we're coming."

"Why not?"

"Because what if Mark or Peter is really Major Matthew Farmer, deserter?"

"Hold on a second." Betsy put the phone down. "Thank you, Mrs. Cooper," she said, handing the woman her change. She waited until Mrs. Cooper was out the door before picking up the phone again. "Jill, do you think that's possible? He'd be a hundred years old!"

"People have been known to live to a hundred."

"Well . . . all right."

"So when do we travel down there?"

"Let me ask the help."

IT was a two-hour journey to New Ulm, a German-themed little city on the banks of the Minnesota River south and west of the Twin Cities.

It was a little after nine, two days later, when Jill and Betsy started down 169 south to Saint Peter, then took 99 west to New Ulm. The air was cool and sweet, and very occasionally a maple tree or sumac bush would be showing just a hint of color. The town had an odd way of naming its numbered streets: 19 South Street, instead of South 19th Street. The first house they went to was owned by a young couple who didn't know any Helga or Matthew Farmer. The second address they went looking for was near the corner of Linden and 6 North Street, in a row of modest clapboard and stucco homes. They all displayed small, well-tended lawns set with dusty lilac bushes and younger trees.

"I bet Dutch elm disease has been through here," noted Jill, theorizing why the trees were all younger than the houses.

"There it is," said Betsy, pointing to a small white clapboard house whose side porch had been glassed in to make an additional room. The place was tidy on the outside, the lawn freshly mowed, but it was in need of a new coat of paint.

They parked and went up on the tiny front porch. After exchanging a glance with Jill, Betsy took a deep breath and rang the doorbell.

The man who answered the door was elderly but not ancient. "Are you Peter Ball?" asked Betsy.

"Yes?" he replied, looking back and forth between the two of them.

"My name is Betsy Devonshire and I'm doing some research on the von Dusen family. Did you used to be married to Helga von Dusen?"

He looked at her for a long few moments before replying, "She was Helga Farmer when I married her. But she's dead now, she died in 1997."

"Yes, I know, but I'm hoping you can tell me something about her. We've been trying to find her for a long time."

"How did you—But here, come on in." He stepped back and gestured at them to go past him into the living room, then followed them in. The room was small and cozy, with fancy crocheted antimacassars on the back of a well-used couch and brown velveteen recliner, and a beautiful, deeply ruffled doily on an end table.

Mr. Ball was short and slim, very bald, with keen blue eyes nearly hidden in a thicket of wrinkles, a long, knobby nose, and too-perfect teeth in a wide, thin mouth. He looked to be somewhere in his later seventies, and he moved a little stiffly—knee problems, thought Betsy—though his fingers were straight and smooth. He was dressed in a faded blue-plaid, short-sleeved cotton shirt, gray twill trousers a size too big, and leather bedroom slippers.

"Sit down, make yourselves comfortable," he invited, gesturing at the couch, upholstered in brown to match the recliner. The three antimacassars on its back displayed a snowy white pattern of pineapples.

Jill and Betsy obeyed, edging behind a blond maple coffee table.

"May I get you something?" he asked. "A cup of coffee, perhaps?"

"No, we had breakfast just a little while ago, thank you," said Betsy.

"Very well," he said and went to sit in the recliner, which seemed to fit him like an old glove. A floor lamp with an angled head peered over the back of it, and Betsy was reminded of the lamp that used to stand behind the upholstered chair in her apartment to light her needlework.

"Now, what was it you wanted to ask me about my wife?" he inquired.

"We're looking for family stories," said Betsy. "For example, how did you meet?" Betsy got a notebook out of her purse and prepared to write in it.

He smiled. "That's a good story. It was in the early fifties. I was the manager of a restaurant in Chicago and she came in when we were about to close. It was winter and her car had broken down. She was cold and tired but without funds to pay for a meal, and my waiter was going to turn her away. She started to cry and I told him to let her stay. I fed her while she waited for the tow truck to come—it took a very long time because the towing orders were all backed up on account of the weather. She had blond hair and a red wool coat that set it off so nice—she was like a movie star. By the time the driver of the tow truck arrived, I had her name and address, and we started to write to each other." He smiled and lifted his arms in a big, happy shrug. "In less than a year I moved to New Ulm—she had this house, you see, and I only had an apartment—and in a few more years I was manager of the Kaiserhof, the finest German restaurant in New Ulm."

"How long were you married?" asked Betsy.

"Only forty-five years," he said with real regret.

Betsy smiled appreciatively at the "only" in his reply. "Did you have children?"

"Yes, a son and three daughters, and now eight grandchildren. They have got their own lives and moved away so I don't see them except two or three times a year."

He was proud to give Betsy their names and addresses, and Betsy was careful to write the information down.

"What did Helga do?"

"She was a receptionist and bookkeeper for a dentist when I met her, and when the children were all in school, she worked as a secretary at Martin Luther College. She was still working there when she had the stroke that took her life." The light went out of his eyes for a moment.

"Is she buried here in New Ulm?"

"Yes, we have a double plot with a double headstone."

Jill said, "You'll pardon me for saying so, Mr. Ball, but how did your wife manage to buy a house on a secretary's salary?"

He looked at her, surprised at the edge he detected in her voice. "She was a widow who owned some lakefront property in northern Minnesota. It was the proceeds of selling that she used to buy this house."

Ball had a precise, almost eloquent, way of speaking that made Betsy wonder where he'd been educated.

"Did you know your wife worked at a German POW

camp up in Cass County during World War Two?" asked Jill. There was still an edge in her voice.

He looked at her for a long moment, frowning very slightly. "Yes," he said at last. "She told me about that. They hired her because she could speak German. She worked for the camp commandant."

Anxious to smooth the harsh edges of the conversation, Betsy said, "There are some wonderful things in this room, beautiful examples of crochet. I'm just learning how to crochet myself, but I can tell these are extremely well done. Did your wife do them?"

Ball turned his face to her and suddenly showed an impish smile. "Every one. Plus more things I have put away. Winters in Minnesota are long and neither of us was much into winter sports, so she and I would sit in this room, I with a book and she with her crochet. Of course, sometimes she would read, too. But I never learned any of the needle arts."

There was a set of shelves against a wall full of well-used books.

"Mr. Ball," said Betsy, "may I change my mind about that coffee? I can smell it and the smell is delicious."

"I do make a good cup of coffee," he said, getting to his feet. "How do you take it?"

"With cream and sugar, I'm afraid. Thank you."

"I take mine black," said Jill.

The moment he was gone from the room, Betsy got up and went to the bookshelves.

"What are you looking for?" asked Jill in a low voice.

"Just testing a theory that you can tell a lot about people by the books they own."

Among the books were modern best-sellers, some biographies, fifties-era books on American, British, and German history, three old books in German—novels by the look of them—a complete works of Shakespeare in one volume, an elderly dictionary, a collection of Norwegian humor—Ole and Lena jokes—and several mystery novels of the noir variety.

"What do they tell you?"

"Nothing much," said Betsy, quickly resuming her seat on the couch, just ahead of Ball's return.

He carried an old wooden tray on which rested three heavy steaming mugs. "Here we are," he said, handing them around before resuming his place in the recliner.

"Were you born in Chicago, Mr. Ball?" asked Jill after taking an approving sip of her coffee.

"No, actually I am English," he replied. "I was born in Canterbury in 1926, and came to America with my parents when I was fifteen."

"*Twenty-six?*" said Betsy. "But that would make you . . . eighty-six years old!"

"Thank you," he said with a pleased nod at her incredulity. "Yes, I am eighty-six and still going strong. I hope to make it to the one century mark."

"I feel sure you will," said Betsy. "Congratulations, and continued good health to you. Now, may we ask you some more questions about Helga?"

"Certainly."

"Do you know anything about how she met and married her first husband?"

"Only what she told me. She grew up on a farm near Longville, Minnesota, and didn't finish high school. She got a job as a waitress and this Army officer used to stop for lunch every day and flirt with her. She started flirting back, fell in love, and against the wishes of her parents, married the man, who was an Army major named Matthew Farmer. He was quite a lot older than she was, and divorced with two or three children, the oldest of whom was nearly as old as she was. It was quite a scandal, I believe, but they were very happy together. He bought a small house on the shore of a lake and she loved it. Then, after they'd been married less than three years, he disappeared. This was during the war. He'd gotten a promotion to lieutenant colonel and orders to someplace in the Pacific, she told me where . . ." He paused to think, then continued, "Sorry, but I don't remember. He was permitted to come home to see her for just a few days, to say good-bye and make sure she had everything she needed while he was gone. She took him to the train depot and he got on the train to Chicago, where he was to take another train to San Francisco. But apparently he never arrived in California, and he was never seen again. She wasn't frightened at first, until several weeks went by without a letter. When he was away from her, he wrote her every week, very faithfully. The Army searched for him and called him a deserter and stopped his pay. What happened to him was never found out, and finally, after seven years, a judge declared him dead."

"What a terribly sad story," said Betsy.

"What did you do during the war?" asked Jill.

"I was drafted into the Army but they found a spot on one of my lungs during boot camp and sent me home. I believe I still have the spot, but it's never given me any trouble. I got a job in a local restaurant as a dishwasher, then was promoted to waiter. My parents were killed in a bus crash when I was twenty. They were poor and could leave me nothing. I was an only child, and all my other relatives were in England, so I was on my own. I went to night school to learn restaurant management, and I was never unemployed right up to when I retired six years ago. The owner of the Kaiserhof, by the way, is two years younger than I am and still working."

"Do you like living in New Ulm?" asked Betsy.

"Yes, very much. The German culture here gets into your blood, I sometimes think I'm as much German as English after all these years." He nodded toward a glass-fronted cabinet. On the top shelf was a narrow-brimmed Bavarian hat with rows of striped cord for a hatband, several medallions shaped like coats of arms attached to the crown, and a hairy feather on one side. "I wear that during Oktoberfest every year, but I gave up wearing lederhosen because I can't dance like I used to."

Betsy smiled and asked in singsong rhythm, "Where did you get that hat?"

He smiled broadly, showing strong white dentures. "Would you believe there's a shop in town that sells them?"

Betsy said, "Well, thank you very much, you've filled in some important gaps in the von Dusen family history." She made a mental vow to contact Larry von Dusen with this information.

They said good-bye and pleased to have met you, and left.

Sixteen

As they got back into Betsy's car, Jill asked, "What do you make of him?"

"He seems like a nice old man who misses his wife."

"Cute story of how they met."

"Yes indeed. Now what?"

"So long as we're here, want to look around? Have you been to New Ulm before?"

"No. I know the owner of the local needlework shop, however. Cindy Hillesheim—I've met her at the Nashville Needlework Market a couple of times. Sweet lady, if a little excitable. I want to see her shop. It's on the main street and has a German name."

"Nadel Kunst," said Jill. "I've been in it."

"Jill!" said Betsy, mock shocked. "You've been going to other needlework shops behind my back!"

"You bet," said Jill. "She has some things you don't have—

just like Stitchville USA does, and for that matter, Needle-work Unlimited and Needlepoint Cottage. Not every shop can have every single thing, though Stitchville comes closest, I think, so far as counted cross-stitch is concerned."

"Well, I never!" said Betsy.

"Oh, I think you have, and probably fairly recently." A corner of Jill's mouth twitched. "Anyway, let's go see Herman the German first. It's such a pretty day, and he's an outdoor attraction."

"Is this a statue we're talking about?"

"Yes, though there's also a structure."

It was Jill being enigmatic, which she did very well. "Okay, tell me how to get there," said Betsy.

"Go up to the corner and turn left and turn left again at the next corner. That's the main street. Then go to Center and turn right."

"Right." Betsy did as directed, and as she drove down Min-nesota Street, they passed a tall rectangle with bells visible in its lifted top. She'd seen churches without a steeple—her own was like that—but never a steeple without a church. "What's that?"

"They call it their Glockenspiel, but I think it's also a carillon."

"I thought a Glockenspiel was one of those Renaissance towers that had figures coming out onto a high stage to strike the bells with a hammer."

"Actually," said Jill, "a glockenspiel is also a xylophone. The word means a lot of things. Watch out, here's Center Street."

Betsy quickly hung a right. In a block or two the street

widened into a boulevard and then climbed a very high hill. At its summit, on the right, was a tall, freestanding cupola on pillars, and on top of the cupola was an immense bronze figure of a man in a short tunic and cape holding a sword over his head.

"Herman the German," said Jill, nodding at the statue as Betsy slowed and turned into a short street leading to a park. She found a small parking lot and pulled in facing the monument.

"Wow," said Betsy. "How big is he anyhow?"

"I think the whole thing is about a hundred feet high, which would make him about twenty-five feet tall, including the sword."

"He looks taller."

"That's probably because of the wings on his helmet." Jill's mouth twitched again.

"Who was he, really?"

"Armanius, to the Romans. In the year nine, over two thousand years ago now, he led his German troops to a great victory over the Roman legions."

Betsy, suddenly enlightened, exclaimed, " 'Quintilius Varus, give me back my legions!' "

Jill said, "*I, Claudius* on PBS, right?"

"Right." Though Betsy remembered reading the book, too, the old television series had been popular viewing back in the 1970s.

They walked around the monument but didn't pay the modest fee to climb the stairs. "What, all those steps for a close-up look at his sandals?" said Betsy. "I don't think so."

And Jill didn't want to climb up alone.

So they headed back to Minnesota Street, found a parking place, and stood for a while on the sidewalk, listening to the pretty music from the Glockenspiel.

"Say, here's the Kaiserhof," said Betsy. The exterior was wood and stucco in imitation half timbering. "I'm hungry and it's lunchtime, so how about we go in? Maybe we'll learn something about Peter Ball that he didn't tell us."

The Kaiserhof had an old-fashioned waiting room with two large murals, one depicting a German-style house and the other the mansion built by Augustus Schell, founder of the local brewery. Down a hallway, the rest of the place had a separate room for the bar, then a series of dining rooms, each decorated slightly differently with half timbers and wainscoting and exposed beams. The place was obviously old, probably dating to the early twentieth century or even earlier.

"I feel like we've walked on a set for a light opera," said Jill, looking around approvingly.

Betsy agreed. "Any minute a set of pretty young women in dirndls will waltz in singing something from *Die Fledermaus*."

Jill had the sauerkraut and ribs, a Kaiserhof specialty; Betsy ordered the German sampler, which included *landjaeger*, ribs, red cabbage, and German-style potato salad. The meals came on big platters.

"You know, the Chamber of Commerce manager in New Ulm is named Sweeney," said Jill with the dead-pan expression that meant she was pulling Betsy's leg.

"Is that a corruption of a German name?" asked Betsy.

"No, it's a Norwegian name that is pronounced something like that, but spelled S-V-E-I-N-E so locals pronounced it

Swine. I understand his father actually changed it to Swee-ney, but the son changed it back again. I guess he's got more patience."

"If he's running the Chamber, he must have." Betsy had done some volunteer work for the Excelsior Chamber and found it a thankless area of local politics.

Their waitress, a college-age woman, had never heard of Peter Ball, and it wasn't until near the end of their meal that an old man came by their table. He was a medium-tall man of stocky build, very friendly, and like Peter, he didn't look his age—he was Mr. Veigel, owner of the Kaiserhof, grand-son of the founder. All he wanted to know was if they had persuaded Peter Ball to come back. "You tell that old man we miss him," he ordered.

The meal finished, they staggered out, replete.

"Look," said Jill, "Nadel Kunst is right across the street."

"I think I can make it that far," panted Betsy, "if we stop for a rest halfway."

They made it and—encouraged by oncoming traffic—without a pause to rest.

Inside, Nadel Kunst was shaped like a capital *L*, with the top of the long upright facing the street. It was packed with shelves and rotating racks loaded with knitting nee-dles and yarn, counted cross-stitch patterns and floss, crochet hooks and fibers, and Hardanger, punch needle, and tatting supplies.

"I bet Helga Ball shopped in here," murmured Betsy, not-ing the many sizes of crochet hooks suspended on a rack.

At the back of the shop was a wooden table cluttered with magazines, patterns, coffee mugs, and an open package of

Oreo cookies. Three women were sitting at the table, knitting. One, a blonde in her forties with a pretty face, rose and came toward them. "How may I help you?" she asked in a surprisingly deep voice.

Jill replied, "Cindy, this is Betsy Devonshire, who owns Crewel World in Excelsior."

"Of course it is! Hello, Betsy! I see you finally decided to accept my invitation to come see my shop!"

"Hi, Cindy. Sorry it took so long. What a nice place you have. I see you know my friend Jill Cross."

"I do know her, yes. So, Jill, what brings you all the way down here from Excelsior again?"

"Actually we came to New Ulm to interview a man named Peter, who used to be married to a woman named Helga."

"Not Peter Ball!" declared Cindy.

"Why, yes, do you know him?"

"He's a very faithful customer!"

"Wait a minute," said Betsy. "You mean his wife was a faithful customer, don't you?"

"I mean dear Peter. He buys all his crochet materials from me."

"Peter Ball crochets?"

"Yes, of course. Did you interview him in his home?"

"Yes, we did," said Betsy, nodding.

"Then surely you saw his magnificent doilies."

"*His?* He said his wife did them."

"Oh? Oh, dear, I wonder if he'll be angry that I told you he made them."

"Why would he lie?" asked Jill sharply.

"Probably because he didn't want to admit that, as a man, he's wonderfully competent at what some would see as a very feminine occupation."

Betsy thought about that. Peter Ball didn't look effeminate, but he was a short, slim man, so maybe he was a bit sensitive about a hobby some would see as delicate, even womanly. And exuberant, lacy doilies weren't the same thing as, say, sweaters or mittens.

"Where did he learn to crochet anyway?" she asked.

"He told me his wife taught him how a long time ago."

"Do you think that's true?" asked Jill.

"Oh, very likely. She was good at most of the needle arts: knitting, crochet, counted cross-stitch—she was a regular customer in here before she died, and taught a class about every other year. But he outshone her at crochet. He's amazing—he can look at a piece for about a minute and copy it perfectly."

"Does he teach classes?" asked Betsy.

"No, he says he wouldn't be any good at that, because he lacks patience. That might be true. I've known other talented stitchers like that."

Betsy nodded and so did Jill. But maybe he didn't want his hobby widely known. "Cindy, would you mind not telling him you told us he crochets?"

"Certainly, if you want me not to."

"Thanks."

Then Betsy noticed the unusual way Cindy had arranged the shelves holding knitting yarn at the back of the shop. Instead of level shelves, the boards had been fastened to the wall diagonally, with more boards going the other way diagonally. This arrangement formed floor-to-ceiling diamond-shaped compartments into which the yarn was laid, each holding a color or weight of its own.

Betsy went back for a closer look. "What a clever set of shelves!" she said. "I may copy that for my shop."

Jill approached the shelves, too, the better to see their contents. "Well, look at this, she has Windy Valley Qiviut yarn!"

Made from the undercoat of musk ox, qiviut was softer and lighter than cashmere and eight times warmer than wool—and far, far more expensive. Each skein, containing 218 yards, weighed only an ounce. She turned to Betsy. "You aren't about to place an order for this, are you?"

Betsy came for a closer look at the stuff. It was the softest yarn she had ever handled, and almost weightless in her hand. Then she saw the price.

"I'm afraid not, unless I get an order in advance."

Cindy said, "I special ordered it for a customer, and she got sick and I held it for her until I'd had it past the return date, then she up and died on me. I can make you a deal on it."

So Jill and Betsy each bought a skein.

Seventeen

T HE next morning, Betsy, back in Excelsior, was in the process of opening up the shop when she found a note on the checkout desk, left by a part-timer yesterday. "Violet Putnam McDonald called. From Longville. Has information about Helga Farmer. Please call." There was a phone number.

Godwin unlocked the front door coming in as she was reading the note, and she waited while he relocked it—it was only nine forty, and the shop didn't open until ten—before holding up the slip of paper and asking, "What do you know about this?"

"What is it?" he asked, coming to take it from her hand. He read the message and said, "I don't know anything about it. I was out on the driving range yesterday, and while your suggestion that I hit a couple hundred balls was an exaggeration, it was not a gross one."

"How's your slice doing?"

"Better than ever," he said glumly. "The more I work on it, the slice-ier it gets."

Yet he didn't sound as depressed as he had when the slice first appeared. "Still want to quit?" she asked.

"Heavens, no!" It was interesting how, although he was impatient with his progress, Godwin was becoming more deeply involved with the game, rather than less. She was not familiar with golf, but she'd seen the same thing happen to novice stitchers, so this phenomenon was not a mystery to her.

"Who is Violet?" he asked Betsy.

"I have no idea. I don't even know how she found out I am interested in Helga Farmer Ball."

"Oh, come on now," teased Godwin. "You who are familiar with the big ol' grapevine under whose shade we in Excelsior cower cannot understand how someone in the even smaller town of Longville might learn of your interest?"

"Well, that's true," sighed Betsy, rembering the woman at the turtle races.

"So, are you going to phone her?"

"Of course."

But there was no answer—nor was there an answering machine, which surprised Betsy. In her experience, nearly everyone had an answering machine.

The mail carrier came in soon after—a new man, who apparently was taking a different route, because usually the mail arrived in the late afternoon.

Betsy sighed over the invoices as she sorted through the envelopes, then paused over a single small envelope without a return address. The envelope was addressed to her at the shop in small block letters. Inside was a three by five card and on it, again in block letters, were two words: LAY OFF.

Godwin saw her staring at it, and came to look over her shoulder. "Oh, my God, a threatening letter! What have you been up to?"

"For heaven's sake, Goddy, you know what I've been up to! This is probably some idiot's idea of a joke." She turned it over and back again. "Or maybe it's the opening salvo of an advertising campaign." But on closer examination, the brief message had been written, not printed on the card.

She reached for the phone and dialed Jill's number. "Has your mail come yet?" she asked. Jill's hadn't, so Betsy said, "When it does, call me. No, I can't talk now, I've got two customers coming in."

They were the Murphy twins and they were brimming over with An Idea. A shop they had visited while on a trip to Canada offered a ten percent discount on any item bought on the customer's birthday, and they had a birthday coming up and what did Betsy think of that idea?

Betsy said she'd think about it, and the twins, who were in their fifties and still dressing alike, left, murmuring in one another's ears, without buying anything.

"So what *do* you think of that idea?" asked Godwin.

"I think it's a good one, but we'll have to ask for proof—and I wonder how many customers would be willing to hand over a driver's license so I can check their age?"

"Oooooh, there's an ugly thought! So let's do it, with a warning that we'll check IDs, because then not everyone will take advantage of it."

"All right, announce it in the next newsletter and on our web site. Thank the Murphy twins for the idea."

Around two, Jill called. "Well, I got my mail," she said. "But why did you ask me to call you when it arrived?"

"Did you receive anything unusual?" Betsy asked.

"No," Jill said. "Did you?"

"Yes, as a matter of fact."

"What was it you got?"

"An anonymous warning." Betsy described it.

"Funny, I don't remember you giving your address to Robert Nowicki."

"I'm in the phone book: Crewel World, Betsy Devonshire, Proprietor. You think it's from Nowicki?"

"Well, I don't think there's been enough time for it to be from Peter Ball. And who else could possibly have sent such a warning? Not Molly Fabrae, she wants us to find out what happened. Can you read the postmark on it?"

Betsy looked at the envelope. "Yes, it was sent from Minneapolis."

"Mr. Nowicki was in Minneapolis a couple of weeks ago looking for a nursing home. Maybe he came back to resume his search."

"But hold on, we wanted to talk to him to find out what he could tell us about the sale of the cabin to his grandparents. That happened more than a year after Dieter Keitel walked away from the camp. What possible connection could his grandparents have to that?"

"None—that we know of."

Betsy ran her fingers through her hair while she thought

about that. "What, you're thinking they might have known one another, the Nowickis and the Farmers?"

"It's possible."

"Oh, Jill, this is ridiculous! All we're getting from our investigation is more possibilities, not fewer!"

"You want to quit?"

Betsy looked at the card with the two words on it: LAY OFF. She was awfully tempted.

"No," she said. "Not yet anyway."

Jill breathed a sigh of relief. "Me, neither," she said.

Betsy said, "Interesting that he sent it to me at the shop. I didn't tell him about Crewel World. And it's kind of a thin threat. 'Lay off,' I mean. Not even an 'Or else.'"

"I think the 'or else' is understood. I'm going to tell Lars about this, and I think you should tell Mike." Mike, as in Sergeant Mike Malloy, one of the two detectives on Excelsior's small police force, the one who knew Betsy and her peculiar habit of getting mixed up in crime.

"All right."

Mike was, as usual, aggravated when he got on the phone with her. "What have you done now?" he growled.

"I decided to help Jill Larson find out how that skeleton came to be in the root cellar of the cabin she and Lars bought up on Thunder Lake."

"Why in the name of all that's holy couldn't you leave it to the sheriff's department up there? They're competent."

"I know, and I'm sorry I'm adding to your law enforcement burden. But this could be an important clue for you—aren't you involved in the investigation, too?"

"No, I'm not. And neither is Lars. It's a Cass County problem. And maybe Stevens County, too, now, since that's where Morris is. Don't handle that card any more than you have to; I'll come by later and take a look at it."

"All right. Thanks, Mike."

Just as she hung up the phone, the door sounded its twin notes, and Betsy turned to greet another customer.

She was a trim senior woman with white and gray hair, cut to fall just over her ears. "Are you Betsy Devonshire?"

"Yes, she is, and I'm Godwin DuLac," replied Godwin. "How may we help you?"

"I'm Violet Putnam McDonald, and I understand you are interested in hearing about Helga von Dusen Farmer."

"Why, I was trying to return your phone call a little while ago," said Betsy.

"I got impatient when you didn't call yesterday and started for here first thing this morning. Wilma Griffin works for the sheriff's department, you know, and she said the sheriff told her you have a reputation for solving crimes, so after I talked with Investigator Mix, I decided you ought to know, too."

"Know what?"

"What I know about Helga. You see, I used to know her."

"You mean, when you were a child?"

"No, I am actually several years older than she is."

"Was," corrected Betsy. "I'm afraid she's dead."

"Oh, dear, dead?"

"Yes, she died fifteen years ago, of a stroke."

"Oh, I'm very sorry to hear that. She was a very sweet girl."

"How well did you know her?"

"We weren't good friends or anything like that. We spoke when we met about what we'd been doing, we exchanged recipes—she had a recipe for pickled green beans that was very good. Things were rationed during the war, of course, so we were always looking for recipes that didn't call for fat or butter."

Godwin said suddenly, "Mock apple pie."

She looked at him in surprise, then smiled. "That's right, made with Ritz Crackers and lemon juice. Not *quite* as good as the real thing, of course, but surprisingly not too bad, if you closed your eyes and dreamed a little. But how do you know about such things?"

"I'm a fan of old-time radio shows, and a lot of the recordings include the commercials." His voice took on a radio announcer's timbre. " '*The Johnson's Wax Program*, starring Fibber McGee and Molly!' "

Violet beamed at him. "Ovaltine sponsored *Little Orphan Annie*, and Jell-O sponsored *Jack Benny*. But who was sponsored by Ritz Crackers?"

"Nobody I know of," replied Godwin, "but when you get interested in an era, you start picking up other things about it. I don't remember where I read about the mock apple pie."

"We're wandering from the topic," said Betsy. "If I bring you a cup of tea, Mrs. McDonald, will you answer some questions I have?"

"Thank you, yes."

In a couple of minutes the women were seated at the library table with a pretty porcelain cup of Earl Grey in front of each of them. "What do you want to know first?" asked Violet.

"Did Helga work at the POW camp in Remer or in Longville?"

"There wasn't a POW camp in Longville."

"Are you sure? Someone described it to me."

"That's why I decided to contact you. There is a *lot* of incorrect information about those camps. Many people mistake the forest sites where the prisoners worked cutting down trees for where they slept at night."

"But she said the ruins had all gone to raspberry bushes and the bears were feasting there to fatten up for winter."

"There is an old logging site that was thick with raspberry bushes for years after the loggers left, but it's gone back to forest now. It was right next to our farm, I can remember hearing the prisoners talking and even singing while they worked."

"Where was the camp where they slept, then?"

"There were three camps, Remer, Bena, and Deer River. Helga worked at the Remer camp."

"Is there a book about these three camps?" asked Betsy. She wasn't willing to say out loud that she didn't know whom to believe.

"I'm sure there must be. I'm speaking from memory, adult memory. The woman you spoke to was a small child during the period the POWs were up there. I'm sure a lot of what she told you is repeated from stories she's heard or even overheard."

"Yes, she said as much. How did Helga come to work at the camp in Remer?"

"She started as a volunteer, teaching the prisoners to knit and crochet. Believe it or not, the men were grateful to her. The three camps used to have competitions in the crafts—

painting, wood carving, needlework—and the Remer camp always walked away with the needlework contest. They also had soccer and boxing competitions, I remember seeing photographs of the teams in our newspaper. Anyway, she had taken a class in typing in school, and when the company clerk proved to be as bad a speller as he was a typist, she volunteered to do that part of his job. Inside of three months, they hired her, and got someone else to teach the boys to knit."

Betsy asked, "Do you remember when Dieter Keitel ran off from the camp?"

"Corporal Keitel is the one they never caught. Yes, I remember there was an awful fuss, just like with the other four. Posters were put up with his picture on it and the sheriff formed a posse that roamed the forest for weeks. The others were found, but not Corporal Keitel. He could speak good English, they said, so they were afraid that if he could get out of the area, he might be able to blend in somewhere. And that's what everyone decided must have happened, that he got to the Twin Cities, or more likely Milwaukee—that city had a large German community—and was taken in by a family. Only now they find these bones and that ID tag, so it seems he never got very far after all."

"How do you think he came to wind up in that root cellar?"

"I'm sure I don't know. If he turned up on their doorstep, the Farmers would have turned him in, and if he put up a fight and was killed, they would have reported it. After all, he was the enemy and Major Farmer was a soldier. His death would hardly be considered murder."

"What did they do, the prisoners?" asked Godwin, who had chosen to re-sort a bin of patterns so he could eavesdrop. "Sit around cooking up escape plans?"

"No, they worked. The Geneva Convention said they could be put to work, so they were. Cutting down trees mostly. But planting them, too, in the summer. And painting public buildings. When the war was over, they were shipped to other camps in Europe. There was some kind of scandal about the French camps, they held them too long or in bad conditions, I forget which. Maybe both. And of course, any that got sent to Russia simply disappeared. Some wanted to stay here, one or two even got engaged to local girls. But they had to go home and apply to immigrate."

"Were they treated all right?" asked Betsy.

"Oh, yes, warm clothing—marked with big black *P* and *W* on the back and legs, of course—and some of them wore pieces of American military uniforms, surplus I guess. Or at least they looked like American Army uniforms with the brass buttons and other insignia taken off. And good food, though after the death camps were found, they wouldn't give them cigarettes anymore and I think they got more potatoes and less meat. Those photographs out of Germany! Some parents wouldn't let their children near the papers if they had those photos in them. But before that happened, they were treated very kindly. People used to wave to them going by in their trucks to the camps where they did the logging. And volunteers came and brought special treats or taught classes. Some of the locals who could speak German were asked to translate—the guards weren't top-drawer, of course; the best of them were overseas getting shot at, poor fellows.

Now I think of it, Helga could speak German; she came from a family, the von Dusens, who spoke German at home. My husband was a farmer with a wife and two little children, so he was exempt from the draft, thank God. But he listened to the radio news every night and followed the progress of the invasion after D-Day on the maps in the newspapers."

"Do you remember Helga's husband?" asked Betsy.

"Major Farmer, the deserter? I don't believe I ever met him, not to talk to. He was stationed somewhere in Wisconsin and came up on the occasional weekend, but of course they were much more interested in staying at home than going out." Violet blushed very lightly.

"Do you remember if Major Farmer's desertion happened around the same time as Corporal Dieter disappeared from the camp?"

Violet thought a long time about that. "No. No, it didn't. Corporal Keitel ran off when it was still summer, and there had been snow on the ground for months when the Army came up here looking for the major." She thought some more. "It was probably the same year, though it might have been early the next, but the two events didn't happen one right after the other. I remember seeing Helga standing in the snow outside the train station, crying because she'd just seen her husband off to combat duty."

"That must have been hard on her."

"Hard on a lot of Army wives—but yes, she was very young, and her husband up to then had served in the support forces stateside. It must have been a shock to both of them when he got orders to report to an overseas location."

"Do you know where his orders would have taken him?"

"No, except it must have been to the Pacific, since he was taking the train to California."

Violet, who was going to spend the night in a motel, was persuaded to cancel her reservation and stay in Betsy's guest room up in her apartment. Betsy called Jill to tell her about Violet, and Jill hinted she'd like to talk with Violet herself and so Betsy invited her to come over after supper.

That evening, Violet sat on the couch stroking a beautiful, overweight, highly pleased cat while Betsy made a soup-and-sandwich supper. Sophie purred and purred; the only time she was happier than when getting unshared attention was when she was eating, and her dinner—a small scoop of Iams Less Active—was long finished.

"All right, Violet, if you will come to the table, the meal—such as it is—is ready." As Violet approached the little round table in the dining nook off the kitchen, Betsy continued, "I'm so glad you were willing to take pot luck with me."

"I'm grateful you invited me. Finding an inexpensive but tasty meal in a strange town is always a chancy thing." She came to the table and said, "Now this looks perfectly delicious."

Betsy had served open-face tuna melts and mugs of tomato soup, with slices of fresh tomato on the side. She believed in setting a pretty table, so there was a small vase of late-summer flowers on the yellow-checked tablecloth.

Because she wanted Jill to take part in any conversation related to Helga Farmer and Dieter Keitel, Betsy asked questions about the Longville area and the little town itself.

"We celebrated the centennial of Longville in 2006," said Violet, "though it wasn't actually incorporated as a village until 1941. It started as a restaurant serving loggers, and then supported a wood pulp factory, though nowadays it's just for tourists and people looking for a summer place 'up north.' "

"It's an attractive town, and that idea of turtle racing was a great one."

"Yes, it's been going on for forty years now."

"It has? I had no idea!"

"Yes, the children who first came are bringing their grand-children to the races nowadays."

With impeccable timing, Jill arrived just as Betsy finished putting the dishes in the sink to soak. She greeted Violet warmly. "I am very glad you drove all that way just to talk to Betsy, and I hope you don't mind my horning in on your conversation."

"Not at all, my dear. I think the more minds we can bring to this conversation, the better."

Jill said, "Oh, Betsy, Lars got a copy of the description issued by the sheriff back when Dieter Keitel first ran off. It includes a picture of him. I thought you might like a look at the man."

"Oooooh, thanks!" said Betsy, reaching for the two sheets of paper Jill was holding out.

The top one was a printout of a jpeg file. The sheriff's department had scanned a wanted poster, complete with photograph. WANTED, it said in big, black letters across the top. Under the word was a black-and-white picture of a very young, thin, scared-looking man with staring pale eyes, a little too much nose, and a wide mouth compressed into liplessness. "Dieter Keitel," ran a paragraph under the photo, "age 20, height five feet six inches, weight 145, speaks good English, a Corporal in the German Army, escaped August 30, 1944, from Remer, Minn. If seen, DO NOT ATTEMPT TO APPREHEND, contact Sheriff Bob Jensen, Walker, Minn."

Violet took a look at the poster and nodded. "I remember seeing this posted in the drugstore, the post office, and the grocery store," she said. "Just like the others."

The second sheet was a doctor's report of a physical examination, describing him in medical terms as undernourished and by his own report inoculated against various diseases. There were blurry fingerprints inked at the bottom. It noted that he had a mole on his left breast and a gold crown on his "30th mandibular molar."

The mole was long gone, but Betsy recalled with fearful clarity the gleam of the gold tooth.

Jill said, "We don't have a photograph of Helga. Can you describe her for us?"

"Well, she was not very tall, but what men called in those days 'curvy,' and what we call full figured today. Not in the least fat, she had a very trim waist, but she . . . well, she was very curvy."

"Was she blond or brunette?" asked Betsy.

"Blond, a very light blond, and natural as far as I could tell. Her hair was thick and probably a little longer than shoulder length—she usually wore it up on top of her head in coronet braids or set in curls. She wasn't just pretty, she was beautiful. She was also sweet and playful and she had a charming habit of speaking rather slowly and looking at you sideways, so some people thought she was slow or even simple-minded. But some of us realized that if you didn't pay attention to her way of speaking but to what she was saying, she wasn't simple at all."

" '*Ein schlaus madchen . . .*' "

"What's that?" asked Violet.

"Something her parents said about her, to the effect that she was a maiden too clever to show how smart she was."

"Yes, that sounds like our Helga, all right. Maybe too clever for her own good."

"What makes you say that?" asked Jill.

"Well, she got that major to marry her, but instead of taking her away from her old life, he abandoned her to it, and in a worse position than when she started."

Eighteen

❈ ❈ ❈

BETSY'S radio alarm went off at five ten the next morning. She reached for it hastily, having no wish to wake her houseguest at such an ungodly hour. Then with a groan— she'd spent a restless night—she slipped out of bed and into a swimsuit. She pulled a loose-fitting dress over it and picked up a zipper bag with her towel, soap, shampoo, deodorant, and underwear in it, packed the night before. She brushed her teeth, combed her hair, left a note for Violet, and slipped down to the small parking lot at the back of her building to take her car eastward to The Courage Center and its Olympic-size, therapeutically heated pool for an hour of water aerobics.

Heidi was the instructor this morning. A trim blond grandmother—Betsy was struck by the notion that nobody looked her age anymore, except, of course, herself—called on the ten women and two men to start a gentle kick while she led them through preliminary stretches.

Soon everyone was jogging briskly while doing "elbow touches," opening and closing their bent arms in front of their chests. "Goooo-od," Heidi crooned at them, though Betsy didn't think she was doing particularly well. Heidi always counted down the last four or five moves before going to the next set, which this morning was a good thing, as Betsy was distracted by tiredness. "Jumping jacks!" called Heidi. "Touch your hands in front, then in back. Ready? Begin!" Betsy sighed and obeyed. But at least the movements were waking her up.

Back home, Betsy found Violet up and in the kitchen, making coffee. "Thank you!" Betsy said and sat down in the dining nook to share a cup with her guest.

"You were very helpful yesterday evening," Betsy continued after a couple of sips. "Thank you. Now, what are your plans for today? I'm sorry I won't be able to take a day off and show you around, but I could take you to lunch."

"Oh, no need of that," said Violet. "If you'll feed me something now, I'll just start right for home."

Betsy wished she could think of a good reason for Violet to stay. Surely there were more questions to be asked— though she couldn't think of any at the moment. "All right," she said at last.

Betsy changed into tailored black slacks and a broad-collared white blouse for work, then the two each had a big glass of orange juice and a bowl of cereal with a scatter of blueberries. Violet thanked Betsy again for the overnight accommodations, then bade her farewell as she went out the building's front door to start her long drive home. Betsy stood waving until her guest turned the corner onto Second Street.

Then walking down the hallway, with Sophie trundling behind, Betsy entered her shop through the back door. She was still feeling tired, but now also discontented with herself. As she went in, she was greeted by the warm fragrance of brewing coffee and stood a moment feeling grateful that Godwin had arrived and started the coffeemaker. The single cup she'd had upstairs wasn't going to be enough to get her up and running this morning.

"*Good* morning, Sunshine!" he called gaily as she came in yawning and rubbing her eyes. "Whoa! What's the matter? Say, did something happen last night, someone trying to make good on that threat?"

"No, everything's fine. I just had a bad night. Stupid dreams and waking up every hour or two. I'll be fine. I'll just take it a little easy today."

"Do that. But you might slip me the high sign if a customer gets on your last nerve, all right?"

"Thanks, Goddy."

A trunk show—actually several sturdy boxes—had come yesterday by FedEx, featuring hand-painted canvases by Sandra Gilmore. Betsy and Godwin spent some time arranging the canvases for display on the library table. They mostly depicted sweet interiors: upholstered chairs with pillows, tables ornamented with porcelain statues and bouquets of flowers, curtained windows, pictures on the walls, all done in soft pastels. A trunk show meant extra work, but also customer interest. They had publicized the show in the shop's newsletter and on its web site. Special prices were offered on the canvases, and often people who came in, drawn by the show, would look around and find other items to buy.

Unfortunately, the last shop to have the show hadn't packed the canvases very carefully, and some were creased. And, Betsy noticed, several others were actually dirty. With her jaw set firmly, she put them aside; she would call the organizer of the trunk show about the damaged items— tomorrow, when she was in a gentler mood.

The phone rang. "Crewel World, Betsy speaking, how may I help you?"

"Betsy, this is Regina Hillerman. The package came with the overdyed silks—but you got it wrong! Really, Betsy, you read the colors back to me and they were right, so I'm at a loss to understand how when I opened the box, three of the colors were not what I asked for."

Betsy was at a loss, too. She'd put the package in the mail yesterday, sure she'd gotten the order right. She took the names of the correct colors again and promised to get them in the mail today. She went to the rack of the silks and very carefully pulled the correct colors, and asked Godwin to package them up now so they'd be ready to go when Fred the mailman came in.

She was looking at the least creased Sandra Gilmore canvas to see if she could perhaps iron it flat, when the phone rang again.

It was Cindy Hillesheim of Nadel Kunst in New Ulm. "Betsy, you know how you asked me not to tell Peter Ball that I told you he is an expert in crochet?"

"Oh, Cindy, you didn't tell him!"

"No, of course I didn't. But I did tell him that you have solved several important murder cases. You didn't say not to tell him that, did you?"

Betsy breathed quietly for a few moments, collecting her temper. "No, I didn't. How did he react to that?"

"Well, he seemed awfully interested, and even more so when I told him Jill used to be a cop. He said that explained a couple of things, but when I assured him that she wasn't a cop anymore, that seemed to tickle him. He said that evidently you can take the badge away from the cop, but not the cop away from the badge. What did he mean by that?"

"Oh, Jill was asking him questions and she came across kind of hard-nosed, I guess."

"What kind of questions? Betsy, are you working on another case?"

"Yes, but that isn't to be shared with anyone."

"Care to tell me about it?"

"No, things are still taking shape and I don't want to talk about it just yet."

"Okay, if you say so. But when you've solved it, will you let me know the story then?"

"Yes, all right." Betsy hung up with a sigh. She wished she'd thought to tell Cindy not to tell anyone she was an amateur sleuth. Maybe it didn't matter this time. After all, Peter Ball was so far out on the periphery of this case, his knowing couldn't hurt anything. Could it?

From there the day began a downhill run. Perhaps it was because she was tired, but there seemed to be more than the usual number of fussy, picky, complaining customers. And one thief. Godwin emitted a shriek when he noticed that someone had slipped away with two needlepoint canvases from the Gilmore collection.

By midafternoon, Betsy had developed a headache behind her left eye that two Advil hadn't been able to displace. It took all her professionalism to remain civil, and the effort left her exhausted.

When at last five o'clock arrived and she could close her doors, she did the minimum close-up routine, sent Godwin off to the bank with the day's deposit, and slowly climbed the stairs to her apartment. Sophie hustled up ahead of her, anxious to get her supper. Betsy had long tried to discourage her customers from slipping fragments of cookie or a corner of a sandwich to the cat, but never with great success. As a result, Sophie's weight usually varied from an obese twenty to a dangerous twenty-four pounds. Betsy fed the cat morning and night, a small amount of Iams Less Active, more to ensure she got a twice-daily dose of something healthy than because she was in need of more calories. Sophie, for her part, always pretended to be famished at the end of a long day of cadging a series of mouthfuls. Today, though, her hunger seemed real, the customers having been in large part not only cranky but stingy.

As Betsy mounted the stairs, the wonderful aroma of cooking food came from one of the other apartments, and she groaned softly, knowing she was in no shape or mood to fix something as delicious for her own supper.

Betsy unlocked the door to her apartment, went into the short hallway, and took the opening on the left that led into her galley kitchen. Sophie trotted ahead of her, crying hungrily in a voice oddly high-pitched for such a massive animal.

Betsy had just finished pouring the little cup of cat food into her dish when she heard a knock at the door. *Dear Lord, yet more trouble?* she sighed as she went to answer it.

Connor, looking as comforting and kind as possible stood there, smiling at her. "Hard day?" he asked.

"Yes, terrible," said Betsy, too tired to offer a polite lie.

"Peg is over in my place, cooking up what you would call a hot dish. Shrimp and mushrooms and three kinds of cheese with peas and pasta in a cream sauce. Only she made more of it than the two of us can eat. Would you care to join us?"

"Oh, it sounds fabulous! But I'm tired and crabby as well as hungry, so maybe I'll pass." Betsy didn't say she also thought she wasn't up to listening to the subtle insults of Connor's grad student daughter without attacking her with something both heavy and frangible.

Going right to the root of the problem, Connor said, "Peg has promised to behave, truly. But since you'll feel braver on your own territory, how about we come over to you? I want her to see that needlepoint piece you're working on—I'm trying to expand her interest in the needle arts. I taught her to knit when she was five, you know."

Betsy had been fifty-five when she learned to knit, and while she was competent at it, she was not the equal of anyone who'd learned as a child. Yet another reason for Peg to look down her nose?

"Oh, Connor . . ."

"Now, *machree*, it's no trouble at all, and you don't look up

to making yourself so much as a peanut butter sandwich."
He was still smiling and seeming very sure of himself. The
apartment door across the wide hall was half open, and the
smells coming from it made Betsy's mouth water.

"Oh, all right. Come on over."

He gave her a swift peck on the cheek and hustled back
to his own place.

In another minute he returned with his intimidatingly
beautiful daughter, she of the dark wavy hair and light gray
eyes. She was carrying a bottle of wine in one hand and a big
salad bowl in the other. Connor was right behind her with a
round casserole dish steaming delectably.

Betsy hurried to bring out three dinner plates, three salad
plates and silverware, and three wineglasses. Peg put the
salad and wine on the table in the dining nook. She picked
up the copy of the wanted poster and the medical report
Betsy had left there.

"Oh, what a sad-looking fellow!" Peg said, looking at the
photograph. Then, "But just a wee moment now," she added,
reading the information. " 'Speaks good English'?"

"He's a German soldier who walked away from a prisoner
of war camp in northern Minnesota in 1944," said Betsy.

The puzzled look on Peg's face cleared. "Ah, this must be
the unfortunate man whose bones were found in the cellar of
a cabin in the north of the state," she said.

"That's right."

Peg looked at the second sheet, eyes moving swiftly over
the two short paragraphs. "This is a pretty cursory physical
examination report."

"They probably figured if he was in the Army, he had already passed a physical."

"Yes, of course."

Betsy had half a loaf of artisan bread, which she contributed to the feast, along with butter. The salad had candied walnuts, dried cranberries, and bits of orange in it; the hot dish was at least as delicious as it smelled. Everyone fell to, and silence reigned for nearly twenty minutes while they all ate their fill.

"The salad I can reconstruct," said Betsy as the meal wound down, "but I would like the recipe for that hot dish, Peg." She was feeling much better.

"All right," said Peg with a pleased smile. "You really do say 'hot dish' here in Minnesota, don't you?"

"I'm afraid so," said Betsy. "Also 'uff da' and 'up at the lake.'"

"Speaking of up at the lake," said Connor, "how's the investigation going?"

"There's not much movement at present," said Betsy. "They've identified the skeleton as Corporal Dieter Keitel, and they suspect he was the victim of a homicide, but the person they would like to talk to about it is dead herself."

"That's too bad," said Peg. "Da says you have an uncommon talent for solving mysteries. I could admire that very much in myself if I had it. Is it innate or did you work to acquire it?"

Betsy touched a place over her left eye where a faint remnant of the headache remained. "Both, I think. It started out as a wild card thing, but experience has made it better. Surely you use detection in the work you're studying to do?"

"Absolutely. In forensic and biological anthropology we study known skeletons to learn to make estimates and predictions about newly found ones. It is like solving a mystery. But you didn't study those subjects, did you?"

For a wonder, this didn't come as an accusation and Betsy was just able to realize that before she took offense.

"No, I didn't. Anyway, I don't solve a murder by looking at the dead person, but by talking with living people who were around him or her."

Connor said, "Tell her about that little case you solved just last week."

Betsy frowned at him. "What case?"

"The case of the unlisted number."

"Oh, that was nothing."

"Tell it anyway."

She sighed, but lightly, and began, "Well, this customer picked up a slip of paper from the library table down in the shop and got all agitated because it was a list of four phone numbers and hers was at the top of the list—and hers is an unlisted number: 555-3346. I managed to get the list out of her hand and saw that the last 'phone number' had only six numbers in it, and I just had to laugh because what she had was a list of DMC floss colors."

"I don't understand," said Peg.

"DMC list its colors by number. The number 555 is for a shade of lavender and 3346 is a shade of green. Someone had brought in a list of floss needed to work a cross-stitch pattern, and left it behind instead of throwing it away." Betsy looked at Connor. "It wasn't a difficult or complicated mystery."

"But clever of you to see what your customer couldn't, though presumably she herself is a cross-stitcher," said Peg.

"I told you she was a *schlauskopf*," Connor said to Peg. "A real 'clever head.'"

Betsy said, "Really, it wasn't anything special at all. But thank you."

Connor said, "May I ask you to show Peg that needlepoint project you're working on?"

"Certainly. But first, let me clear the table. Would you like a cup of black tea or coffee or cocoa?"

"Oh, coffee, please, thank you," said Peg.

"Me, too," said Connor.

"I'll put the coffeemaker to work. Why don't you make yourselves comfortable in the living room? This won't take a moment."

In a few minutes Betsy brought two cups of fragrant brew to her guests and then brought out the stand to which her needlepoint project was fastened. It was a Melissa Shirley tapestry called "Circus Bear," and it depicted, in a style to delight a child, a brown bear on all fours wearing a green and red birthday paper hat and a pink ruffled saddle, being ridden by a long-tailed monkey in a harem costume. She was working it in Hungarian ground, pavilion diamonds, and bargello stitches, among others, with the background in the stitcher's basic basketweave.

Peg broke into a smile when she saw it. "How sweet!" she exclaimed.

Betsy showed Peg how the basketweave stitch was done and allowed her to complete a row, which she did with no problem. But Betsy could tell Peg was displaying good manners rather than a real interest in the technique, so she put the stand away.

When she came back, she found that Peg had picked up the wanted poster and physician's report again.

"You're studying biological anthropology at the university," said Betsy, "so I imagine you are reading all sorts of interesting things in that report I wouldn't understand."

"Perhaps, but you saw the actual skeleton, didn't you?" said Peg. "I am discovering that I'm much more a hands-on person than a document person."

Betsy said, "I knew a forensics person who claimed she sometimes got hints about who a person was by just handling their skull. Her work was putting faces back on them, in a manner of speaking, of course—and she said the dead sometimes would tell her things, like the color of their eyes or how they wore their hair."

"It's a psychic gift." Peg nodded. "I know of other people who have it. I'm not sure if I have it or not. I just know that it's exciting to find a skeleton or set of skeletons where they were laid down, either angrily or with love and grief. Such finds can tell us a great deal about the living folk who put them there."

"I think I can see what is drawing you to such a profession."

Peg looked askance at Betsy. "I don't suppose you believe in ghosts?"

Betsy smiled. "Yes, I do. I've actually seen one or two in my life. But I don't have the gift of calling to them or hearing their attempts at communication." Betsy returned the slantwise look. "Do you?"

"Believe in ghosts? I wouldn't be a true daughter of Ireland if I didn't! But bones and ghosts are two different things, and I'm less sure about what bones might have to say. Perhaps it's because I've so little experience with them and so I don't know how to listen yet, but it could be I haven't the gift at all." For the first time, Betsy felt a liveliness in Peg, a deep stir of interest in a topic. Maybe it was because they were talking about something Peg really knew a lot about.

Betsy said, "I remember a feeling of awe when I saw those bones. I didn't handle them, of course, I only looked. I do remember seeing the gold tooth gleaming under the dust, and that made the humanity of the bones apparent. I could suddenly feel that those dusty old bones used to be an actual person. But it was more interesting to me to see that photograph, to see an actual face."

"So the jaw hadn't rolled away when it came loose from the skull," said Peg.

Betsy was puzzled. "Yes, it had. It was upside down in a scatter of ribs."

"But you saw the gold tooth in it."

"I saw a gold tooth in the upper jaw."

Peg frowned at her. "But it says the gold crown is in the lower jaw."

"It does?"

Peg touched her chin. "This is the mandible. If the crown were in the upper set of teeth, it would have said maxillary."

Betsy stared at her. "But the gold tooth I saw *was* in the upper jaw—the maxillary."

"Then something's wrong. The doctor—and he probably was a doctor, this is very physician-like language—said a gold crown on a right mandibular molar. That's here." Peg touched the right side of her jaw, working the joint back and forth.

Betsy felt a curious sort of electrical current running from her elbows to her fingertips. "You're sure?"

"Of course I'm sure."

"That's very interesting. No, it's *terribly* interesting, and important. I want to tell someone right away what you've told me. Will you excuse me a minute?"

"Of course," said Peg.

Betsy hurried into the kitchen to call Jill. She repeated the conversation she'd just had with Peg, concluding, "Tell Lars he'd better contact that investigator up in Walker right away. The skeleton might not be Dieter Keitel's after all."

Betsy went back to the living room, feeling a shaky smile pulling at her mouth. "Peg, you've just done the most fantastic thing! You've broken a homicide case wide open!"

Peg said, "I can't believe people in charge of the investigation read that description and didn't realize where that gold crown was located."

"I'm sure the sheriff back then knew it was in the lower jaw, and I'm sure there were other documents that pointed it out. This came about because all we have are two documents, and it didn't say 'lower jaw' on the wanted poster, and none of the few modern-day folk who read the doctor's description understood it. I'm so glad you picked that up. You're the hero of the day, for sure!"

Peg's face was glowing and her smile was wide. Her father looked proud.

But now, of course, the question standing up with a hand raised was—if not Dieter Keitel's, whose bones were they in that root cellar?

Nineteen

Betsy thought she was in for another bad night. She was excited about this break in the case and her mind puzzled over the unstable way the known facts butted up against this new one. If the skeleton was not Dieter Keitel's, what was his identification tag doing in the cellar?

Was Dieter Keitel the murderer, not the victim?

Who was the victim? Could it be Matthew Farmer? That would explain why he never turned up in San Francisco.

But wait, wasn't he seen getting on the train to Chicago?

And what about the civilian-style buttons instead of military brass?

Betsy crawled into bed prepared to think things over, but the moment she closed her eyes, she fell asleep.

And she woke the next morning feeling refreshed and energized—and with a new idea. Well, not exactly a new idea. She showered and dressed, then got onto the Internet to check her e-mails and read a couple of newsgroups. She sent an e-mail to Jill:

Hello to Emma Beth and Airey [because they loved getting messages handed along from their mother's computer] *and good morning to you. All right, at long last I feel we might have a grip on this thing. I now believe Robert Nowicki, or some other member of his family (of course he told them all about his adventure in Excelsior as soon as he got home) sent that 4 X 5 card warning me to Lay Off. Because it's now likely the skeleton belongs to Robert Nowicki's missing Uncle Jerry, poor fellow. That he was put down in that root cellar by Robert's grandparents. As soon as you hear what the sheriff's department up in Walker is going to do with the case, let me know, all right? I can't believe we all were so stupid about that mandible business. Have a super day!*

She sent it, read some messages on RCTN, replied to a couple of e-mails, and shut her computer down.

She set her books on the dining noon table so she wouldn't forget to take them downstairs—her accountant was due in this morning to check her records, reconcile her bank account, and take the payroll figures to write paychecks. Then she went into her kitchen to prepare her breakfast and feed her cat.

It had taken months of determined effort, but she had managed to move the cat's breakfast feeding time back from "right after the morning trip to the bathroom" to "when I have my own breakfast." Sophie still complained about it, but Betsy refused to budge or feel guilty. Bad enough that the cat's current weight was a morbidly obese twenty-two pounds.

Not that Sophie waddled or showed other symptoms of

discomfort at that weight. She was a large, heavy-boned cat with long fur, mostly white, with a cap of tan and gray that extended down her back and up her tail. She was beautiful, graceful, and had no apparent metabolism at all. At one time Betsy had gotten her weight down to seventeen pounds, but had become alarmed at the meager amount of food it took to keep her at that weight—and her customers, who took to slipping Sophie bits and pieces of food as part of their Crewel World shopping experience, grumbled, so she released her strict control. Sophie put on three pounds in two months. Her vet sighed and said she seemed otherwise healthy, so that was that.

But Betsy kept a needlepointed sign that said, NO, THANKS, I'M ON A DIET, on display on the back of Sophie's favorite chair. Her customers cooperated by sneaking food to the cat rather than feeding her openly, and Sophie did her part by hiding her erratic and dangerous snacking habit.

Betsy looked with exasperated affection at her pet, who was licking the bottom of her bowl with a raspy tongue, helping along the pretense that this was all she'd have to eat until the shop closed that evening.

Then the two of them went downstairs to open up.

Godwin came in right at ten, making a comedy of peering around the edge of the open front door as if afraid of the mood he might find his boss in. Betsy's laugh reassured him that yesterday's gloom was gone and he came in with a laugh of his own.

"Rafael said you'd be better this morning," said Godwin, "but I wasn't so sure."

"Was I so awful yesterday?" asked Betsy.

"My dear, you were perfectly dreadful." Godwin's smile remained. "Almost as bad as I was about this time last year when we thought it was never going to stop raining. Remember?"

"You weren't crabby, you were depressed."

"It amounts to the same thing as far as I can see. I did thank you for being patient with me, didn't I?"

"Yes, and you were wonderful yesterday. Thank you. Let me tell you something that happened last night."

"Strewth!" Godwin exclaimed when he learned that the skeleton was not Dieter Keitel's—but he leaped to Betsy's overnight conclusion before she could tell him about it.

"It's that missing runaway uncle's, isn't it?" he said. "Have you told the Cass County sheriff about this yet?"

"No, Jill's doing that, probably right now. Like it or not, Max Nowicki is going to have to talk to them about his parents."

"So it looks as if you've solved another one," said Godwin. "How many does that make?"

"I don't know, Goddy, I don't keep track."

"But you should. Start a journal. Someday you'll want to write your memoirs, *My Forty Years as a Sleuth*."

Betsy laughed. "Forty years? Do you know how old I'll be in forty years?"

"Maybe ten years older than you are right now," said Godwin, and he went away to turn the shop sign to OPEN.

Soon after opening up, Sergeant Mike Malloy called to say the only fingerprints on the four by five "Lay Off" card he had taken away were Betsy's. "Morris PD went and had a little talk with Robert Nowicki about it," continued Mike. "He denied all knowledge of it, of course, but Sergeant Philips reported he was scared and angry. Philips thinks he put the fear of God into Nowicki, and now the man knows we're on to him, that'll likely be the last threat you'll get."

"Thanks, Mike," said Betsy. "Have you talked with Jill or Lars yet this morning?"

"No, why?"

Betsy told him about the break in the case that had occurred yesterday evening. "Jill is going, if she hasn't already, to talk with Investigator Mix up in Cass County," she concluded.

"Maxillary or *what?*" Mike asked.

"Mandibular."

"Well, who knew?"

"Nobody we know, that's for sure. Except Peg Sullivan."

"Hell's bells, this is ridiculous!"

"No, it probably means that missing teen, Jerry Nowicki, is who the skeleton belongs to."

"Maybe. Maybe. How about, just for once, we don't go leaping to a conclusion?" suggested Mike. "Let's see what Cass County makes of those bones now." He hung up.

For some reason, the customers today seemed much calmer, friendlier, and happier than yesterday. Their questions seemed less like whining, their demands not at all annoying. And nobody stole anything.

Around three, Jill came in with her two children, and a couple of flat packages. The bigger one contained a counted cross-stitch pattern of two realistic black-and-white loons— well, three; one of the loons had a fluffy baby riding on its back. The pattern was worked on a piece of fine linen dyed in mottled shades of deep blue and violet. The effect was as if it were twilight, when sky and water are the same dark color.

It was the Paula Minkebige pattern from the Crossed Wing Collection that Jill had purchased just a few weeks ago.

Emma Beth said, "I won't cry when the loons sing a sad song anymore."

"She says she wants this hung in her bedroom," said Jill.

"Not up at the cabin?" asked Betsy.

"Up at the lake are real loons," said Emma Beth.

"I told her we had to have it properly finished before we hang it up anywhere," said Jill.

"It's beautiful," said Betsy. To Emma Beth she added, "I'm sure it will look beautiful in your room."

"I helped stitch it," said Emma Beth proudly.

Betsy looked at the tiny crosses on the dark fabric.

"Mama let me pull the needle lots of times," she added.

"I see. Well, the stitching is very well done, you did a good job." Lots of women encouraged an early start to stitching by allowing even very young children to pull a needle, once started, through the fabric.

"She was surprisingly persistent," said Jill with a wry smile. "She'd work for up to half an hour with me on this piece."

"I can stitch real good," said Emma Beth.

"You stitch very well, darling. I think that very soon we're going to have to start you on your own plastic canvas."

Betsy and Jill discussed the possible colors of mats and styles of frame for the loon piece—with some input from Emma Beth. Airey showed his own talent for patience through it all. Jill said, "We're going to go look at puppies if he's good."

"I be *good*," Airey declared.

The finishing decisions made, Jill said, "Now, this other package is for you. Good luck with it."

When she and the children were gone, Betsy opened the package to find a cardboard-stiffened brown envelope. Inside that were six color photographs of a human skull, a full face, right and left profiles, and right and left quarter profiles. In several of them a gold crown on an upper molar was visible.

Godwin, coming for a look, said, "Is that real?"

"Yes, it's what we thought was the skull of Dieter Keitel."

"And now is known to belong to Jerry Nowicki."

"Mike says not to leap to another conclusion. I'm pretty sure the sheriff of Cass County has a way of finding out. Probably dental records exist, he can check them. But there are other ways."

"Like what?"

"He can get a face put on these bones." Betsy stared at the photographs. "I've heard forensics departments generally have a severe backlog of work so that's likely to take a while. I wish I didn't have to wait for them. Hmmm, I may have a way of getting it done faster for myself."

"Don't you have to have the actual skull to do that?" asked Godwin, remembering how it was done in a case some years back.

"I know it's usually done with a computer nowadays, instead of a person laying clay down on the skull with the aid of markers they glue on. I'm hoping all we need is photographs. I'm going to call Connor."

"You think he knows?"

"No, but his daughter does."

Connor promised to ask his daughter to call Betsy as soon as he could get hold of her, which he thought was likely to be this afternoon, unless she was doing some lab work.

Betsy was helping Godwin compare the contents of an order from Norden Crafts against her original order form when the phone rang. "Crewel World, Betsy speaking, how may I help you?" she said on picking up the phone.

"Betsy, this is Peg Sullivan. Da said you wanted to speak with me?"

"Oh, yes, thank you for calling so promptly! I have the most audacious favor to ask of you."

"What is it?"

"Remember how you pointed out that, by the description, the skeleton we found couldn't be Dieter Keitel's? Well, I have a set of six very clear photographs of the skull and I'm wondering if you know someone who could put a face on one of them, working just from the photographs."

There was a thoughtful little silence. "It can be done," she said at last. "I'm taking a class on how to do it this semester."

"I was hoping you would say that."

Peg laughed. "I'll come over this evening, all right?"

"Thank you."

Peg came over around seven. "Hmmmm," she said, looking them over swiftly. And going through them again, more slowly, "Hmmmmm." There was an eager, almost greedy, look on her face. Her mouth opened and Betsy thought she was actually going to lick her lips.

Betsy asked, "Does the ruler in the photographs help?"

"Not really; it's the proportions between features that tell you the shape of the face. These are excellent photographs.

May I borrow the wanted poster with Dieter Keitel's picture on it?"

"Certainly. How long will this take?"

"Possibly as long as a week."

But Betsy got a phone call the following afternoon. "Well, it isn't Dieter Keitel's skull."

"I thought we knew that."

"What we had was a description that didn't match. I made an overlay of Keitel's face on the skull and it doesn't fit. The placement of the eyes, the shape of the mouth, the nose—it doesn't fit."

"So now what?"

"Now I try to make a face that does fit. Betsy, thank you for calling me about this. I am really looking forward to doing something . . . something *real*. I hope I don't disappoint you—and myself."

"I'm sure you won't."

Twenty

❖ ❖ ❖

JILL was adamant: "No more investigating up in Cass County. They're on it now," she said. "And if we butt in the wrong way, we could hurt the case they're building. Plus we could generate some ill will that I don't think Lars and I need, since we're going to be spending time up there in the cabin."

So Betsy gritted her teeth and agreed. But it was hard. She felt she was hot on the trail to the solution.

Jill called the next day, Friday. "Did you get something in the mail today?" she asked.

"Just the usual. Why, what did you get?"

"Another of those three by five cards. Mine says 'STOP SLEUTHING' in all capital letters."

Betsy was so shocked and frightened she could only think of banalities in response. "Terse fellow, isn't he?"

"Yes. I've called Mike Malloy, he's on his way over."

"I thought they had this stopped," Betsy said. "What do you think we should do?"

"Well, first of all, I sent Lars to take the children to Gram and Grampa Larson until we get this figured out."

"Yes, that's imperative. What can you tell about the card?"

"Not much. I think it's just like the one you got."

"What's the postmark?"

"Same as before: Minneapolis."

"Jill—"

"No, I don't think we should quit." This was quite a change from her statement the previous day. Jill sounded sure to the point of anger about it.

After they hung up, Betsy sat at the checkout desk for a while, thinking. Mike had sounded awfully sure that Robert Nowicki had received the message to stop writing threatening notes. Of course, Betsy was getting the report from Mike, who had it from someone in the Morris Police Department, who had it from Robert. Who knew how that message had changed over the course of being handed down? She did understand that Robert had strongly denied he was responsible for the notes.

Could that be true? What if Robert hadn't written them? Maybe it was Max of the shattered cheekbone sending them. Maybe it wasn't the Nowicki family at all.

Since there were no customers in the shop, Betsy reached into the carpetbag under the desk and pulled out her knitting. She had long ago found that knitting a simple pattern, as of a knit two, purl two scarf, was a way to free her mind of anxiety and clarify her thoughts. She was currently working on one in Christmas colors of red and green. In a minute or two she could feel her pulse slow and her thinking become more coherent.

But sadly, no new ideas formed.

IT was Sunday, only three days since Betsy gave the photographs of the skull and the wanted poster to Peg Sullivan. She had just come home from church and was deep into English muffins and jam and her second cup of black tea with milk and sugar when there was a knock on her door.

With a sigh over her interrupted breakfast, Betsy went to answer it.

Peg stood at the door, with a big smile on her face. "I've got it!" she said. "May I come in and show you?"

"You have it already?" replied Betsy, stepping back and waving Peg in.

"Professor Johnson let me turn it into a project for credit," she said. "So I could take the time to really focus on it. The face I got looks like a real person, almost. At least as much of one as I could make it. It's hard to resist the temptation to ignore some clue the skull is giving you in order to make the face more realistic. And of course, there's the problem of not having the basic talent for drawing to do this really well." Peg's smile had been becoming more and more apologetic as she spoke. "Plus, without being able to handle the skull, I wasn't sure what age he was. But anyway, I have a face to show you."

Betsy led the way into the living room, where she took the envelope Peg was carrying and said, "Let's have a look."

The envelope was held shut with a big paper clip, which Betsy slid off. Inside were three sheets of paper, an original and two photocopies. Behind them were the six photographs of the skull.

The original, a pencil drawing, was just the head of a man in his forties with a thick head of dark hair cropped short on the sides. His jaw was square, his nose short and a little broad, his eyes large and set well apart, light-colored and intelligent. His mouth was wide and heavy, the artist trying for a sensual effect that didn't quite come off.

"This is really interesting," said Betsy. "It looks like a real person."

"As drawn by an amateur," said Peg.

"Well, not all that amateur, and it looks more as if it were drawn from life than from measurements taken from a skull."

"Thank you," said Peg, wriggling just a little with pleasure. "My professor thought it adequate and accurate."

Betsy could not take her eyes off the face. *Who are you?* she thought. The eyes looked back at her, but enigmatically. She reached for the full-front photograph of the skull, and managed to shift her attention to it for a few moments. Nothing about it, to her, suggested the face in the drawing.

"How sure are you that what you've done really represents the person who used to occupy this skull?" she asked Peg.

"There's been a lot of research done on this," Peg replied. "There are rules about the placement of the eyes, the shape of the nose, the width of the mouth, and the thickness of the flesh on the bone that apply to every human, so once you know them, you can get a good estimate of the basic shape of any face. Of course, if a person is thin or fat, that will affect that shape, and age brings about changes, too. You told Da that Major Farmer was years older than his wife, that he'd been married before and had a son old enough to join the Army, so I made him middle-aged."

Betsy stared at her. "I didn't say I thought the skull belonged to Major Farmer!"

Peg said, dismayed, "No? Oh, no! But—but who else could it be?"

"I don't know, not for sure. But it's not the major. I've got two separate reports that Helga was seen at the train station saying good-bye to her husband as he left for California. I do have reason to believe the skeleton was put down there by the next owners of the cabin, Marsha and Arnold Nowicki. And that the person in the cellar is their sixteen-year-old son, Jerry."

"I don't understand. What makes you think that?"

"I got a threat, warning me to stop investigating, and the only person who would send it is Robert Nowicki." Betsy explained about the interview with Robert.

"Well, now, isn't that interesting," Peg said.

"Yes, so I'm pretty sure it's the missing boy."

Peg reached out, took back her drawing, and looked at it again. "And I was so sure I had it right. Do you want me to redo the sketch?"

Betsy looked at the drawing. Was it what Jerry would have looked like in middle age, had he survived? Maybe she should ask Peg to redo the drawing, making the face that of a very young man. Even so, just getting this glimpse of the face made her wish all the harder to put the final pieces of the puzzle together.

O N Monday at two, the Monday Bunch came into session. A group of mostly senior women stitchers, they met one afternoon a week to do needlework and gossip. Emily was one exception to the group's demographic—she was not yet thirty—and Phil was the other. He was a retired railroad engineer. All of the Bunch were avid supporters of Betsy's efforts in the field of sleuthing.

So Betsy felt free to show them the pencil sketch Peg had done, putting a face on the skull found in the root cellar.

Godwin, who had seen it earlier, said, "I think he looks like a nice man."

"I think he looks kind but bossy," said Patricia.

"Let me see," said Emily, putting down her knitting. She took the sketch and looked at it, holding it first close up, then at arm's length. "I agree with Goddy, he looks like a nice man."

But when Phil looked at the sketch, he merely shook his head. "He looks like one of those mealy-mouthed college professors to me."

"You think so?" said Betsy, surprised.

"Or an office manager, a paper pusher," said Phil, nodding, and he handed the sketch to his wife, Doris, an attractive woman in her sixties, with curly hair dyed a cheerful red.

She studied the drawing briefly then said, "I think that in

real life he was sexy." She handed the sheet to Alice, a tall, strongly built woman with a chin not to be trifled with.

"His mouth is all wrong," she pronounced. "Who drew this?"

"Connor's daughter Peg," said Betsy. "She's a forensic anthropologist, not an artist."

"I can tell she's no artist. Still . . ." She tilted the sketch from side to side. "I can tell he was a handsome man, with a good sense of humor, but there was something wrong with him in his . . . manliness."

Betsy was amazed at what the Bunch was reading into an amateur pencil sketch.

Bershada was last to look at the sketch.

"Nice looking," she said at first. "But weak." She glanced at Alice. "Not womanly, and not a crook, but weak as a man."

Alice nodded, and Betsy said, "I am surprised you are able to decipher this man's personality just by looking at a drawing of his face."

"Oh, come on!" said Godwin. "We all do that all the time. We look at someone's face and decide right away if we should stay or walk away—or run."

"All right, I understand that, but we make those decisions based on what years of living have done to the muscles and skin of the person. This is a reconstruction of a face based just on his skull. We have no idea what living did to the muscles."

"Bad to the bone," said Bershada with a little laugh.

"No, I think he was nice," said Godwin. "I'd've liked to be friends with him."

"So would I," said Betsy.

"Have you gotten any more threatening notes?" asked Phil.

"No," said Betsy. "But Jill has."

That created an unhappy sensation around the table.

"I think you should drop this," said Alice.

"Jill doesn't want to," said Betsy. "But she has sent the children away until the person who mailed the notes is discovered and arrested."

"Good idea," said Phil, and the others nodded.

"We know who sent them," said Godwin, "but we can't prove it. He's very clever and left no fingerprints and he wrote with block letters, which you can't compare to his usual handwriting."

"So who did send them?" asked Bershada.

Betsy replied, "Right now, I suspect a member of the Nowicki family. Marsha and Arnold Nowicki were the next owners of the cabin after Helga and Matthew Farmer. It's possible the skeleton belongs to their teenaged son, Jerry."

That created another, very satisfactory sensation. Godwin nodded. "It's possible this is Jerry Nowicki, as he would look if he'd lived to middle age instead of dying when he was only sixteen."

"So why did the Farmers run away?" asked Alice.

"That's a good question," said Betsy. "I'm thinking now that the rumors about the two of them from back in the 1940s might be true. Major Farmer got orders for overseas duty and deserted in the face of those orders, and then, when he got established somewhere new, with a new identity, he sent for her."

"So they're still alive?" asked Emily.

"Probably not. Major Farmer was a lot older than his wife, so he's likely deceased. And we know Helga Farmer died of a stroke some years back. Seven years after he disappeared, a judge declared him dead, and sometime after that she met and married Peter Ball, and they ended up living in New Ulm. Then fifteen years ago she died of a stroke."

"Could this Peter Ball really be Major Farmer?" asked Phil.

"No," said Betsy. "He's in his eighties, but very spry. Major Farmer would be over a hundred years old. For another, he's not an American, he was born in England . . ." She paused, frowning.

"What?" asked Godwin.

"Something . . . I don't know." She smiled. "He's not like you, Phil. He can crochet circles around many of us, but he's ashamed to admit he can do it at all."

"Nothing wrong with crochet!" said Phil, lifting the cup cover he was working on. "If it wasn't for needlework, I wouldn't have met and married Doris." He gave her a fond smile, and she smiled back at him.

Nice, thought Betsy, that some people find happiness in each other. She thought of Connor, and her smile was not dissimilar to Doris and Phil's.

The door sounded its two notes and a woman in late middle age came in. Her hair was brown streaked with blond. She was dressed all in gray with touches of red: a long gray skirt with a red flower embroidered on the hem, a gray sleeveless blouse with red piping, gray sneakers with red shoelaces, and a red cardigan. She was carrying a gray string purse with a red lining showing through. After a moment, Betsy said, "Hello, Molly. What brings you out?"

"You do." She looked at the people sitting at the table and Betsy said, "Come with me," and led her into the back of the shop. "Would you care to sit down? I can bring you a cup of tea."

"No, I'm not staying long. Betsy, have you learned anything at all?"

Betsy first offered an apology for the real problem. "I'm sorry I haven't contacted you. It's just that we don't seem to be making any progress. Everything is still just questions, and more questions, and all I learn leads to still more questions. Except we know that the skeleton isn't that of Dieter Keitel but someone who was killed after your father and stepmother moved away. But we don't know who it belongs to." Betsy made a gesture of frustration. "Everything is fragments and speculation! I wish there was a chain of evidence going from the start right through to today! But there isn't. I'm really sorry, I'm starting to think we'll never solve this."

Molly turned away and put her face in her hands. "This isn't fair," she murmured, and Betsy came to rest her hands on the woman's shoulders.

"I know, I know. I *wish* there were something else concrete I could tell you. Well, wait, there's one thing, but it's just another fragment. We got hold of some photographs of the skull and I have a contact in a forensic anthropology class at the university. She put a face on the skull—but it's not right, it should be a young face, and she put an older man's face on it. It's out on the table, if you want to take a look."

"Thank you," said Molly without enthusiasm, but she turned and went out into the front area.

"Here it is," said Betsy, picking up the pencil sketch and handing it to her.

Molly took it, gave a little scream, and fell to the floor.

They soon had Molly sitting in a chair with her head down between her knees. She began murmuring something and Betsy knelt down to hear what it was.

"Please let me up," was what she was saying. "Please let me up, I'm all right now."

So Betsy lifted her upright. Her head lolled and she was so pale that her makeup—which hadn't even been visible when she came in—now looked almost clownish. But she repeated, "I'm all right, really, I'm all right."

"Would you like something to drink?" asked Godwin.

"I'd really like . . . Just some water, please."

He hurried off to the back room.

"What happened?" asked Betsy. "You didn't look ill when you came in."

"It's that drawing," said Molly. "It's my father's face."

"*What?*" Betsy turned and picked it up off the carpet where Molly had dropped it. "Your father? Are you sure?"

Molly smiled a strange smile and nodded. "He had one of those very thin mustaches, they're called 'pencil mustaches' because they look like they're drawn on with an eyebrow pencil, but otherwise it looks just like him."

"Strewth!" exclaimed Godwin, coming back with a bottle of chilled water. "Your *father*? But I thought we had eyewitnesses to him getting on the train! Helga was crying in the snow and everything because he was going away to war!" He unscrewed the cap and handed the bottled water to her. He said to Betsy, "This changes everything, doesn't it?"

Betsy felt a wan smile pull at her mouth. "Again. Yes, it does." She looked at the pencil drawing in her hand. "Peg said she made the man middle aged because she thought I'd said it might be Matthew Farmer."

Godwin stared at her then gave a dramatic shudder. "Oh, wow, that is just too strange, too, too strange!" He came to look around Betsy's shoulder at the drawing. "That's what Major Matthew Farmer looked like? So who was Helga seeing off on the train?"

Twenty-one

❈ ❈ ❈

"So then that means . . ." said Jill a couple of hours later. She and the children were sitting in the dining nook in Betsy's apartment. The puppy she had promised the children was ready for pickup, so she had "borrowed" them back from their grandparents for the afternoon. The initial squealing, hugging, chasing, and other means of getting acquainted were over, and everyone could draw a calming breath for at least a little while. Airey was eating Cheerios, O by O, from a little bowl; Emma Beth was drawing with crayons on a sheet of typing paper.

On the floor under the table was a black dog about the size of an adult cocker spaniel, but without the big, pendulous ears and with a long, thick tail and enormous feet. It was busy eating the Cheerios that Airey had dropped, moving with the eager clumsiness that marked it as a puppy.

Sophie had withdrawn to her basket in the living room from whence she could keep an appalled and wary eye on the intruder.

"It's possible," said Betsy. "He's the right age and size."

"But what about the gold tooth? Peter Ball didn't have one."

Betsy thought back to the little old man in his living room full of beautiful doilies. He had a wide smile—and perfect, very white teeth. No one in his eighties could have natural teeth like that.

"Dentures," said Betsy. "He's got dentures now."

"All right," said Jill. "But how do we prove it?"

"I don't know. Go talk to him, I guess."

"What if he's got a gun? He's been making threats."

"Unspecific ones. Almost meek ones."

Betsy said, "I'm not so sure he's meek. He's clever, after all. And energetic—he must have driven up to the Cities to mail those threats, so they wouldn't have a New Ulm postmark. I think maybe the threats were terse for fear we'd find something about the writing that would point to him."

"Oh. Yes, you're right. Actually, I wonder now why he wrote at all. Didn't he think we'd go to the police?"

"That depends on what Cindy told him. If she said I was an amateur sleuth, then he'd think I work cases without the aid of the police."

Jill nodded. "I'll bet he has no idea that Cass County and Hennepin County law enforcement know you're working on the case. When he finds out, he may try to run."

"At age eighty-six? Where will he run to? What will he do when he gets there? What will he live on? He'll have to abandon his house and any savings, and even his Social Security checks."

"Yes, poor fellow," said Jill in a very dry voice.

"So you think he won't run."

"If he murdered Matthew Farmer, I hope he does run. I hope he winds up in a musty, dark cellar somewhere, with lots of spiders for company, and an old jar of green beans for sustenance. He's had a good life: a wife, children, grandchildren, an honorable occupation, respect in his community, far and away more than he deserved for taking a man's life. Not to mention the hell he put Matthew's daughter through."

Betsy was a little startled at the vehemence in Jill's voice. Normally a very cool head, here her words had hot, sharp teeth in them.

"All right, you're right. So what should we do? Go down and see if we can set him on the run?"

"Arf!" said the puppy. Airey had run out of Cheerios.

"Hush, Bjorn," said Jill. "No, at this point, I think we need to have a conference with Mike Malloy and Investigator Mix." Mix was the Cass County Sheriff's Department investigator.

Betsy went into the kitchen to get the box of Cheerios and pour just a little into the bowl in front of Airey. "Nice!" he said, and immediately dropped one on the floor for the pup.

"Can you say thank you?" asked Jill.

"Thank you," said Emma Beth, selecting a black crayon to make a scribble she hoped would turn out looking like Bjorn.

"Fan' 'oo," said Airey, putting a Cheerio into his mouth, chewing twice, and grinning messily at Betsy.

"You're welcome, darling," said Betsy.

*　　*　　*

Oɴ the drive up to Cass County on Wednesday morning, Betsy asked Jill, "Why a Newfoundland? Aren't they really, really big dogs?"

"Yes, the males can go thirty inches high at the shoulder and as much as a hundred and fifty pounds. But they are gentle and they love children—and without any training at all, they will go into a river or lake and rescue a drowning person. Since both our home and our cabin are on a lake, we thought that was a splendid feature. Did you know the big dog in *Peter Pan* is a Newfie, not a Saint Bernard? The Victorians loved them because they guarded children and were endlessly patient with them."

"Are you going to have Bjorn trained as a guard dog?"

"Oh, no, they aren't really good at that. Their idea of protecting their families is to stand between them and whatever they perceive as a threat. They don't growl or bite or even bark a whole lot and so long as they are permitted to go swimming in the summer, they are, overall, happy campers."

"Yeah, but he'll eat you out of house and home. I mean, a hundred and fifty pounds? He'll eat half a cow a week!"

"No, they're thrifty keepers once they reach full size. Because they're lazy. One long walk a day is all they need. I want to see if he'll go cross-country skiing this winter. In the summer, they sleep in the shade."

"All right, I give up, he sounds like a good match for you. Where did you get the name *Bjorn* for him?"

"Bear is a very common name for the breed. And *Bjorn* is Norwegian for 'Bear.'"

Going to Walker, the county seat, added a little over an hour beyond the length of a trip to the cabin. Walker was an attractive little city on the shore of Minnesota's biggest lake, Leech Lake. To judge by the false-front brick buildings, it was probably the same age as Excelsior. The County Courthouse, which also held the jail and sheriff's department offices, was a stately brick-and-white-marble edifice on top of a low hill on the edge of downtown.

Investigator Mix was summoned by a sheriff's deputy sitting on the other side of a slab of bulletproof glass. He came out and shook their hands and led them through a locked door back to his small office. There, he seated them in front of his cluttered desk, got them each a mug of bad coffee, and then phoned Mike Malloy back in Excelsior. Once connected, he put Malloy on his speakerphone and said, "Hi, Sergeant Mike Malloy, glad you could join us via phone. I want to state at the outset that our conversation is being recorded, okay?"

"Sure," said Mike.

Since Investigator Mix's statement was intended for Jill and Betsy, too, they each agreed. "Yes, that's fine," said Betsy.

"Yessir," said Jill.

"I will also note for the record that it is eleven forty a.m. on Wednesday, August twenty-eight, that present in my office are Elizabeth Devonshire and Jill Cross Larson, both civilians of Excelsior, Minnesota. This is in regard to an active homicide investigation." Mix went on to describe in brief terms the discovery of the skeleton and its positive identification as one Corporal Dieter Keitel, of the German Army, brought to Cass County as a prisoner of war in 1944. "Later information indicated that it might not, in fact, be Dieter Keitel's skeleton but some other person's.

"Now, you two women are here to say that the skeleton is that of the owner of the cabin, Major Matthew Farmer, is that correct?"

"Yessir," said Jill.

"What makes you say that?"

Betsy got out the pencil sketch and handed it to Mix. "Jill was given a set of photographs of the skull of the skeleton. She brought them to me, and I asked an acquaintance to see if she could put a face on the skull using forensic techniques. She could, and here is the result. It has been identified positively by his daughter as the face of Major Farmer." Betsy reached again into her large purse and brought out a photograph, which she handed across. "This is a photograph of Major Farmer loaned to me by his daughter. I think the resemblance is remarkable; the only thing Peg Sullivan missed was that skinny little mustache." The photograph, a formal portrait that measured five by seven inches, depicted Major Farmer in his dress uniform, complete with hat, so it was impossible to tell if Peg had gotten the hair right.

"I don't know if you know that there are eyewitness accounts of Helga Farmer seeing her husband off on the train in November of 1944."

"Yes," said Betsy, nodding, "I have spoken with Violet McDonald, who was at the train station that morning. She did not actually see Major Farmer board the train; if she had, I think she might have been surprised to see that he'd shrunk an inch or so and lost some weight."

"How is that?" asked Mix.

"I think the person she put on that train was Dieter Keitel, who rode on Major Farmer's ticket only as far as Chicago. He wore the major's uniform and carried the major's suitcase. The major lay dead in the root cellar, his body partly covered by the POW clothes and ID badge that had belonged to Dieter."

Mix sat back in his chair, which creaked loudly in protest. "I think I need more details than what you've given me so far." He was looking at Jill, who said to Betsy, "You start."

"Helga von Dusen grew up in a family that spoke German at home, so it was her first language. Her parents were old-fashioned in many ways. As the baby of the family, she was told that she would never marry, but would have to stay at home to take care of them in their old age. They even pulled her out of high school, probably to remove the temptation of boys her own age. But they weren't ready to retire just yet and they let her get a part-time job as a waitress. And there she met an Army major, in town to inspect the pulpwood factory making cardboard boxes for the military. They fell in love and, against her parents' wishes, married."

Jill took up the tale. "The major was not a wealthy man; he was divorced and paying a good portion of his income in alimony and child support. So he bought a modest home for his new bride, an old log cabin, and soon afterward put her on the deed as co-owner. He was stationed at Camp McCoy in Wisconsin, working in supply, and would only get home on occasional weekends—his work at the Longville pulpwood plant soon ended. Because of that, and because he was an outsider, he was not well known in the area."

Betsy continued with the story. "Helga soon had the cabin

in good order. She planted a garden and canned vegetables from it, storing them on plank shelves down in a root cellar under the cabin. She probably bought cordwood; she was a small woman, sturdy but not strong, and not able to cut down, cut apart, and split all the wood it would take to cook with and heat the cabin during the winter.

"In 1944, a troop of almost five hundred German prisoners of war, most of them from the North African campaign, were brought to a revamped CCC camp in Remer. It was manned by a handful of soldiers with a 'shavetail' lieutenant in charge. A few local civilians were hired, and other locals came as volunteers, bringing food and supplies such as basketballs, soccer balls—which must have been rare and hard to find back in that era—boxing gloves, and so forth. Volunteers who could speak German were especially prized, and Helga was one of them. She taught needle crafts to the prisoners. When it became evident that she could type better than the Army clerk assigned to the task, she volunteered to assist him—and proved so valuable she was hired as the camp commandant's secretary. Sometime during that period, she met a prisoner named Dieter Keitel. He was a lowly corporal and just nineteen years old. But Helga was eighteen, lonely, bored, and vulnerable."

Jill said, "There were very few escapes from the camp, and the men who tried walking away were rapidly caught. Except one, Corporal Keitel. That's because he had a place to go, a place where he could hide in comfort. It's a little hard to use the term 'mistress' with regard to Helga, because it suggests that the man is taking care of the woman, and in this case she was taking care of him. They were lovers, however, young and passionate, making foolish promises, I have no doubt. When visitors—or possibly even her husband—came to the cabin, he hid in the root cellar."

Betsy said, "But Major Farmer got unexpected orders to the Pacific. He was to take a train to the Presidio in San Francisco, and a troop ship from Naval Air Station Alameda. He had only a few days to prepare, and decided to go home to tell his wife in person, and make sure she had everything she needed to get through the coming winter without him. This wasn't a regularly scheduled visit and he did not telephone or send a telegram before coming up—the cabin did not have a telephone, so he would have had to leave word at Brigham's store. He figured it would be a pleasant surprise. Well, it was a surprise, all right, but not a pleasant one. He walked in on his wife and her lover, and there was a terrible scene. Either immediately, or upon learning that Dieter was a POW, he attacked him. During the fight, someone, Helga or Dieter, picked up something heavy and clouted Matthew on the head—twice."

"Now," said Jill, "the fat was truly in the fire. What were they to do? Matthew was dead. Who had he told he was going home? His commanding officer knew—and would send someone looking for him. I don't know which of them got the idea, but it was a good one. They stripped Matthew of his uniform and Dieter tried it on. It wasn't a good fit, but Helga could fix that with her sewing skills. They put his body down in the root cellar along with Dieter's prison clothing—that's why there were only plastic buttons in the cellar, not brass ones. And when the time came for Matthew to take the train, they drove in that big old Auburn automobile, and Dieter, well wrapped up against the snow in the major's uniform, got on the train. He got off in Chicago and disappeared into the crowd. Helga's frightened tears, which were witnessed by Violet Putnam McDonald, were very likely genuine. But she pulled herself together, drove home, and the next day ordered a roll of linoleum for the cabin floor. When the Army came looking for Major Farmer some weeks later, all they found were his worried wife and some reports of seeing her putting her husband on the train. He was marked down as a deserter, but was never found, nor did he turn himself in. In 1945, Helga sold the cabin to Marsha and Arnold Nowicki, and moved away."

"Six years later," said Betsy, "the major was declared dead by a judge. Helga had meanwhile moved to New Ulm, where she put a substantial down payment on a modest house and got a job as a secretary. She took her secondhand car on a jaunt to Chicago, where it allegedly suffered a breakdown. It was a cold winter night when she walked into a restaurant seeking a phone to call a tow company. A waiter didn't want her to wait in the place because she didn't plan to purchase a meal. The manager of the place, a Peter Ball, not only let her stay, he fed her. By the time the tow company arrived, he had her name and address. They began a correspondence. It warmed into a relationship and then a courtship. In the end, Peter moved to New Ulm to live with his bride in her modest house. They were very happy, raising a boy and three girls, and ending up with eight grandchildren. He wound up managing the Kaiserhof restaurant, and she became secretary to one of the deans at the New Ulm

Christian College. They were very happy until, after forty-five years of marriage, she suffered a stroke at work and died."

The two women fell silent. Mix looked at them, one then the other. "So Dieter gets away and Helga is dead," he said. "The case ends there?"

"Oh," said Betsy, "didn't we tell you? Dieter *is* Peter. He had learned English from an Englishman, so he could pass as someone who came to America from England as a teen. It must have been difficult those first years, working menial jobs while he built an identity, scrubbing the last of his German accent away. Then, very carefully, and only after it was safe, they arranged to meet in Chicago. Living in New Ulm, with a wife who spoke fluent German, he could let the remnants of his German attitude and even the occasional German phrase show and explain that under the circumstances it was hard not to become a little bit German himself."

Jill whistled a phrase from an English music hall song, and Betsy nodded. "But he forgot to make himself more of an Englishman. When we first spoke with him, I pointed to a Bavarian hat he owned and asked, in the phrase of probably the best-known English music hall song, 'Where did you get that hat?' and he took it as a legitimate question. Didn't crack a smile. It didn't really bother me—I suppose there are living Englishmen who are unfamiliar with the song—until I started putting the pieces of the puzzle together and it became another small piece."

Jill said, raising her voice, "It was Peter who sent those threatening notes, Mike. He went over to Nadel Kunst after we talked with him, and the owner, Cindy Hillesheim, told him Betsy was an amateur sleuth who didn't work with the police on a case. About scared the bejesus out of him, probably. He thought we came to see him because we were researching Helga von Dusen—and we were, of course. So he went to the drugstore and bought a box of new envelopes and a packet of three by five cards, took them home, and wearing gloves, prepared that brief warning. Then he drove all the way to Minneapolis and dropped it off at a post office in time for the last pickup."

"Mail can be delivered in a day in the Twin Cities area, it's a terrific service," said Betsy. "I'd forgotten that until I got a phone call from a customer who got a package with a mistake in its contents that I'd mailed to her the day before. Poor old fellow must have worn himself out getting that done and up to the Cities in just a few hours."

Jill said, "I think, Betsy, we've already had a conversation about feeling sorry for that murderer."

"Yes, you're right. You know, it was clever of him to have done that, so it makes me wonder if it wasn't his idea to use the major's train ticket and uniform to get away. But no, Helga had her own reputation as a *schlauenkopf*, so maybe not."

"The question now is," said Jill, "how do we smoke Herr Dieter out?"

Twenty-two

❖ ❖ ❖

JILL and Betsy sat in Betsy's Buick across the street from Peter Ball's house. In front of the house were two New Ulm squad cars and an unmarked police car that Investigator Mix had driven down from Walker, stopping in Excelsior to pick up Mike Malloy on the way.

The two women were there on sufferance, having no official role to play and under strict orders to stay in the car.

A New Ulm police officer knocked on the door. There was no answer. Peter Ball's car was in the driveway; he should have been at home. The officer knocked again, harder, and this time announced himself: "Police Department, open the door!" Jill and Betsy could hear him all the way across the street.

"What's wrong, why doesn't he answer?" asked Betsy.

"He's scared, probably," replied Jill. "I wonder if he hasn't been expecting them to come knocking? I mean, did he think we'd come in person?"

"I don't know."

"Look, they're going in."

The door wasn't locked. The little group of men were cautiously entering the house. The New Ulm police officers had their hands on their guns, but hadn't drawn them. They left the door open.

After a wait, Betsy realized she was holding her breath. She deliberately let it out and drew another deep one.

Then she heard a siren.

"Calling for backup?" asked Betsy.

"No, that's an ambulance."

"Oh, no, do you think they've hurt him?"

"I don't know," Jill replied. She sounded very calm—but then Jill usually did.

A police officer came out onto the porch and waved at them. When he saw he had their attention, he gestured at them to come over.

Up on the porch he said, "Try not to touch anything, all right?"

"What's the matter?" asked Betsy.

"We want you to identify Mr. Ball," he said, and led the way through the living room into the kitchen.

It was a small room, done in shades of tan and green, its style dating to the sixties but with a center island. On the island's far side lay Peter Ball. He was surrounded by pots and pans and also by what, after a moment, Betsy identified as a ceiling rack designed to hold the utensils suspended. Ball was not moving, and the back and side of his head was a mess of dried blood. A cast-iron frying pan on the floor nearby had dark red smears along its edge.

One of Ball's legs was caught up in a three-step stool that had fallen over.

Investigator Mix said, "Is this man Peter Ball?"

"Yes," said Betsy.

"Yes," said Jill.

IN the shop the next morning, it was very quiet. Though the phrase "not your fault" echoed in Betsy's mind—and in truth, what happened to Peter Ball was not anyone's fault, except, perhaps, the person who'd installed the pot rack— she felt that somehow she had brought Nemesis into the little old man's life.

She and Jill.

And maybe Molly Fabrae.

And maybe Peter himself, for climbing up on that wobbly old stool to reach for a pot or a pan? whispered a voice from the back of her mind.

Maybe.

But Mike had called Betsy at home this morning to say that Peter had fractured his skull in two places and broken his arm in the accident that killed him, probably the evening before he was found. "Old men's bones break easy," Mike had noted. "And their balance isn't always very good. A pure accident, but a heck of a coincidence that the injuries that killed him are the same as what killed Matthew Farmer."

Yes, thought Betsy. *A heck of a coincidence.*

And she thought again of Molly Fabrae.

Shortly after lunch, Jill came in, and Betsy told her what she'd been thinking. "It's making me a little sick," she said.

"I thought about it, too," said Jill, "and I checked it out. I called Molly to tell her about finding Peter Ball in his kitchen. I thought, How would Betsy ask for an alibi in a way that wouldn't warn her subject? So I said, 'It makes you think, doesn't it? I was home making supper for Lars and the children when it happened.' And it worked—Molly said she'd spent the whole afternoon with her three grandchildren, buying them back-to-school clothes, then had the family over for pizza. The party didn't break up until nearly nine."

Betsy sighed in relief. "I'm so glad. I feel terribly sorry for her, but at least that one sad part of her life has an ending. How's Bjorn doing?"

"He didn't have an accident last night, but actually waited until I let him out this morning. He'll do."

After Jill left, Godwin came over and said, "How are you feeling?"

"I felt so sorry for Mr. Ball, and now he's dead."

"Anything I can do to help?"

"I'm afraid not. I'll get over it. Jill thinks it's poetic justice, and for all we know, it is."

"Is that what's bothering you? That you don't know for sure that he killed Major Farmer?"

"Well, I'm sure that either he or Helga did it. But yes, I guess I'm thinking that it's possible he was just a horrified spectator at the major's death."

"No, no, no," said Godwin. "Think about it. Dieter and Helga are heavily—culpably—involved with each other late one evening when in walks the husband. Whether Matthew goes for his wife first or Dieter, it was the other who came to his or her defense. There was probably a big three-way battle going on before one or the other grabbed the frying pan and started swinging. Can't you just see it? Matthew threw his arm up to defend himself and smash! It's broken, he turns away yelling, and gets smacked a good one on the back of his head."

Betsy, grimacing furiously, shouted, "Stop it, stop it!"

"But that's probably how it happened," said Godwin in a reasonable voice. "Except I can't explain that second fracture."

Betsy put both hands on her face. "I can," she said in a muffled voice. "The major didn't die at once, but was so horribly injured they decided to finish the job."

"Ugh!" said Godwin. "You're worse—or do I mean better?—than I am at thinking up awful scenes."

"That's why I hate to think about them. They're horrible and so vivid in my mind that I hate starting them."

"Well, then, let's think about something else. My golf game, for example. Or the fall window display."

"Yes, let's."

But before they could pull out the file folder with the window design in it, the door sounded its two notes and in walked two women. One, Ann Mobius, Betsy knew. "I'm going to be a grandmother at last!" she announced. "I want a birth announcement! Oh, this is Sandy Sechrest, who doesn't stitch."

Sandy said, "But I do collect needlework. Have you got any finished pieces for sale?" She was a short woman, a trifle plump, with white hair and interested blue eyes—they were looking through the opening between the box shelves at the walls in back covered with framed needlework.

"I'm afraid not," said Betsy. "These are models, to show my customers what a finished piece of counted cross-stitch looks like."

"Beautiful, they're just beautiful."

"She's just retired from her job as a librarian at the University of Wisconsin at La Crosse," said Ann, who was a tall woman, deeply tanned, with dark hair and eyes. "So now she has the time, maybe we could interest her in a beginner pattern."

"No, thank you," said Sandy with a laugh and a dismissive gesture. "I've got enough projects already lined up. You go ahead and look for your baby pattern, I'll just sit out here and wait." Sandy went to the library table, took a seat, and got out her Kindle. "Finally," she said to Betsy, "time enough to read all the books I want to read."

Betsy smiled and nodded and went to help Ann select a pattern and the fabric for a birth announcement.

Ann said, "What's this I hear about the police making an arrest in that strange case of the skeleton in the root cellar?" She chuckled. "That sounds like a Nancy Drew mystery title, doesn't it?"

"Yes, it does," said Betsy. "Here, these are the birth announcements. Will you need fabric?"

THAT evening Betsy went to Connor's apartment for supper with him and his daughter. Peg was still cock-a-hoop over having broken the case by putting an identifiable face on the skull, but also a little nervous at having her desire to be psychic proven true. "Me heart is still all kerfuffled," is how she put it, fluttering her long fingers on her chest.

Connor was beaming at her from the couch, Betsy sitting beside him, his arm flung carelessly around her shoulders. "Ah, *machree*," he said to her, "I know you were all anyhow while working on this case, but it's a long road without a turning in it, and I'm glad for all our sakes that there was a solution at the end."

"Yes, but it's too bad about Mr. Ball—Mr. Keitel, I suppose I should say."

"No, Mr. Ball suits him better; after all, he spent most of his life as Peter Ball. I suppose after a while he must have come close to forgetting he was ever Dieter Keitel."

But Betsy shuddered just a little, remembering the scenario Godwin had evoked of the murder scene in the cabin. Who could forget that? Surely there must have been bad dreams on some nights. Perhaps in late autumn, when the first snow fell . . .

She snuggled a bit closer to Connor, and he responded by stroking her shoulder.

Was the murder worth it for Dieter and Helga? Was getting your heart's desire enough?

She didn't know.

Shooting Stars

A Dusty Rose Original Pattern
Designed by Alixandra Jordan

- Model stitched on black Aida 14 count using 3 strand DMC cotton and 2 strand DMC Metallic
- Backstitching for Shooting Stars done in 2 strand silver DMC Metallic
- Star buttons from Just Another Button Company™

Area	Symbol	DMC	Anchor	Description
Trunk	•	3799	236	Pewter Gray—very dark
Branches	O	561	212	Jade—very dark
	X	319	218	Pistachio Green—very dark
	+	987	244	Forest Green—dark
Shoreline	Z	934	682	Black Avocado Green
Water	E	336	150	Navy Blue

Shooting Stars

Area	Symbol	DMC	Anchor	Description
	A	5283		Metallic Silver
Stars	A	5283		Metallic Silver
		or		or
		White	2	White

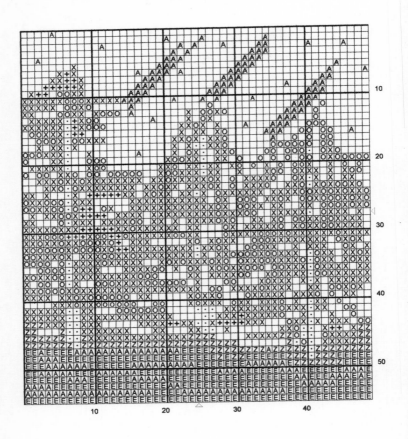